GOD DAMN THE UNION!

GOD DAMN THE UNION!

by

Cole Rickard

Dales Large Print Books
Long Preston, North Yorkshire,
England.

British Library Cataloguing in Publication Data.

Rickard, Cole
  God damn the union!

  A catalogue record for this book is
  available from the British Library

  ISBN 1-85389-704-3 pbk

First published in Great Britain by Robert Hale Ltd., 1995

Published in Large Print 1997 by arrangement with Robert
Hale Ltd.

Dales Large Print is an imprint of
Library Magna Books Ltd.
Printed and bound in Great Britain by
T.J. International Ltd., Cornwall, PL28 8RW.

ONE

Captain Brad Corman, lately of the First Texas Cavalry—and a bundle of grey, war-torn rags today—stiffened in his saddle and lifted a shielding hand to his eyes. There was smoke on the skyline ahead, black, pluming clouds of it, and his heart hardened as the old bitterness of conflict gathered within him anew. That was a burning town over there. What was more, it looked like his own hometown of Raftville, north Texas. God damn the Union! Would it never stop? All these weeks after the surrender at Appomattox—and the Yankees were still burning and pillaging in the defeated South. It made a man doubt that there was any good left in human nature. War surely did unspeakable things to people!

Lifting his bit and momentarily breaking his mount's gait, Corman heaved up in his stirrups and hoped to glimpse something more where the fireclouds seethed, but there was just the smoke over there and the falling horizon, with the aching miles in between and all the promise of spring in the carpets of daisies and other wild flowers that traced the plain towards the big sky of the burgeoning year. Yes, it was a fine sight—and one after which Corman had long yearned—but those fingers of hell on the morning blue had taken his joy and filled him with a sickening apprehension.

Dropping back into his seat, Corman let the rowels fly and put on pace, stilling his mind to some extent and concentrating on the ride between here and Raftville, which he figured would require about thirty minutes to complete. Now he went along evenly, boring at the faint pressure of the breeze and conscious of the increasing stink of his mount's sweat and the ache of a backside which recent semi-starvation and four years of rough riding at the head of his troop had reduced to little more than twin blades of bone that the flesh barely protected any longer from the jolting frictions of a weathered saddle which was falling into black decay. 'Son, it will last many a year,' his now dead father had told him, when making the saddle as a twenty-first birthday gift; and so it had; but now, fourteen years later and with the War Between the States intervening, it was a torment and an eyesore that the much-matured Corman intended to replace at the first moment that he had some cash money to spare.

The skyline fled southwards as the galloping Corman chased it back, and presently the captain went at it harder still. He was now approaching the low ridge which, earlier undetected in the green flow of the greater vista, had to some extent obscured his view down country. His horse coughed and sighed, playing the patient one under this recently unaccustomed pressure—since it had been a long ride from Virginia and Corman had naturally spared it all he could—but now it was all stretch and thunder again, with the spurs biting at softened hide which the dash of battle had once kept hard.

They topped the brief climb, and the south rolled before them, more splendid yet, with the sun standing tall as it neared the zenith and a haze dimming far crags to the west that came and went. Now the clouds of smoke, mere hanging portents not so long ago, were a baleful presence, puffing and jerking in a life of their own, the acrid stench of their soot an offence to tongue and nostrils alike, and Corman sat as he saw that what he had feared was indeed the case, for Raftville was blazing sullenly here and there along its straggling length and an unseen pall of despair confirmed yet another episode of misery in a life that seemed to have become an unbroken tragedy ever since April 12th 1861 had dawned.

Moving down the land now, but at a much slower rate, Corman headed into the northeastern fringe of the burning town. His house was nearby, and he held down all thought and emotion until he was sure that it still stood. Yes, it occupied its little bench as securely as ever—though he could see traces of smoke twisting out of his open front door—and he feared at once for the recently married wife whom he had left in the place four years ago, since she ought to have been visible and doing what she could about those hints of fire. Yet there was something unreal in everything present. It was like gazing at the once familiar through the dilapidations of a nightmare. The crooked chimney, peeling shutters, and unkempt garden seemed to wail at him of a neglect that was symptomatic of a further grief to come. Anne! Why hadn't she been more prominent in his thoughts this morning? Had the devil himself been saving up to produce a special impact? Yet it could be explained simply enough; for with only the weak memories of those brief days of marriage to recall, the girl had never become what most husbands would regard as a habit of mind. His love for her throughout the war had been more theoretical than of the bone.

Reining to a halt outside his front gate, Corman swung down, aware of people beyond him—and of frantic activity and much else—but for now he had no interest in what was taking place elsewhere and, flinging open the gate, raced for the house, torn skirts of his coat flapping and a sole loose on one of his boots. 'Anne!' he shouted, determined to do all in his power to protect and save—and feeling guilty too; for how could he almost have forgotten about his beautiful, wayward, unpredictable, sharp-tongued wife when the presence of disaster had been written so large upon the earth ahead? Good God! She might even be dead! He was an affront even to himself!

'Anne, darling!' Into the house he went, knowing of a thousand horrors that could have occurred and praying aloud that all was still well with her. 'Anne! It's me, Brad! I'm home, darling!'

There was no reply. All he heard was the faint crackling sound made by the small yellow flames that were creeping along the skirting boards on either side of the hall and producing the curls of smoke which he had seen just now as he had approached the house on horseback. Again he shouted his wife's name, and once more the hush mocked him. Perhaps Anne wasn't here. Maybe it was no worse than that. She could well have gone to seek a hiding place elsewhere when disaster had struck the town. He must get a grip on himself, and think calmly. As always, first things must come first. He must see to the house before any severe burning occurred. This was home—the future. If future there was to be.

Corman hared down the hall. He entered the kitchen at the back of the house. The pantry was situated on his left. Jerking open the door, he put his head and shoulders into the little room, picking up the bucket of drinking water which stood under the lowest of the provision shelves on his right. Carrying the bucket at arm's-length, he re-entered the hall and went round the skirting boards, putting out all the fire present in a minute or so.

Then, blowing momentarily, the captain set the now empty bucket on the floor. After that, on the chance that his wife could be lying unconscious in one of the main rooms or that more fire might have been set elsewhere, Corman began a quick but thorough search of the dwelling. He went from the parlour to the bedrooms and, though he suspected that a few items of value were missing, he found nothing to worry him further. Calming down, he left the house a short time later—confident that his worst fears were not to be realized here—and, with his home saved, he felt free to seek any information to be had concerning his wife's whereabouts.

Making his way back to the front gate, he rejoined his horse and stood at the animal's head, looking down the fire-lined main street of Raftville towards a spot where folk were clustered around a pair of bodies on the ground. There was the probability that somebody yonder would have the information he needed, and be able to tell him what exactly had happened to his hometown earlier in the day. Best get

13

along there, but leave his mount behind. The stallion was a big brute, and would only get in the way where troubled folk were jostling.

Corman tied his horse to the picket fence adjacent. Then he walked down the slight incline before him into the town proper, stopping within that knot of people who were gathered around the two bodies. Heat gusted at him from a nearby fire, and he felt like kicking a dog that kept yelping and whining to itself, but pity possessed him as he saw a yellow-haired girl who was weeping heartbrokenly to herself while crouched against one of the verandah uprights at the front of Rufus Lebeau's Black Boot saloon. He was of the mind to go to her, and offer what consolation he could, when a man's face turned round and up at him, its strong, blocky features showing a moment's surprise and then lighting up with sheer pleasure. 'Well, I do declare! If it ain't that son-of-a-gun, Brad Corman, come home at last!'

'Hello, Frank,' Corman returned, recognising the other—a trifle more grey-haired and ample than when last seen—as Frank Jessup, the town baker, a shrewd and knowing man if ever there'd been one, and his late father's best friend. 'What happened here?'

Misunderstanding the wider import of the question, Jessup evidently thought that Corman was asking after the two people, old folk and clearly dead, who lay in the dust not a yard beyond them. 'Isaac and Louie Forbes,' the baker explained, spitting tobacco juice at a fragment of fiery wood as it flew past his head. 'Shot through. Dead as they come.'

'I can see that,' Corman responded, perceiving then that the blonde girl crouched a short distance away was Mary Forbes, the grandchild whom the old couple had brought up and who had been little more than a teenager when Corman had left for Richmond and the war. 'Poor Mary!'

'Poor everybody!' Jessup echoed grimly.

'So who did it? When exactly did it happen?'

'Couple of hours back—around ten o'clock.'

'Two hours ago!' Corman snorted, unreasonably angry. 'Have you folk been standing round that dead couple ever since?'

'Don't talk so damned silly, Corman!'

15

an unnoticed listener at Jessup's left elbow flared. 'We've all been hidden up. Isaac and Louie Forbes would still be alive if they had taken proper cover. They had warning. Everybody was given warning.'

Corman turned his gaze on to the new speaker, a well-dressed, full-bellied man, with a small-featured, rubicund face, intelligent black eyes, and pink baldness betrayed all the way around the brim of his derby hat. He never had liked the other—Rufus Lebeau himself, saloonkeeper, usurer, and man with a finger in many pies for miles about—and he liked him a lot less now, since a captain of cavalry didn't have it suggested too often that he was a damned fool. 'So you've been hiding up, Rufus, and encouraging everybody else to do the same. Figures.'

'Don't you use that tone of voice on me, Corman!' Lebeau warned, nodding in acknowledgement of the threatening growls which rose from the throat of a truly huge man who stood opposite him. 'You always were your father's son and shared his worst characteristics. Sam Corman was all mouth and very little brain too.'

'A coward is a coward in any language,' Corman said bluntly. 'But he doesn't have

16

to encourage others to be cowards too. We have to fight for what's ours.'

'That's what you've been doing, isn't it?' Lebeau sneered. 'And look where it's got you. You're a scarecrow, man—a scarecrow!'

With a great effort, Corman subdued his fury. He always strove to be fair, and there had been a grain of truth in what Lebeau had just said. He had been fighting for ideals and a way of life that he had long ago come to doubt. No man had the right to own another—much less to fight for that right—and the South had been growing effete on slavery and fortunes in black flesh. 'I take it this was a Yankee raid?'

Lebeau shrugged. 'Is there something new in that?'

'I was at the surrender,' Corman said. 'I heard General Grant warn that there was to be no more of that. The Yankees are on pain of death. If you'd fought back here, you'd have done so with Grant's blessing.'

'General Grant is a long way off, Brad,' Frank Jessup reminded, 'and we've no law to turn to. The Southern Judiciary has been wiped clean by Washington. All we've got is a darkie police force, and them coloured men are mostly down Fort Worth and Dallas way. Besides, our raiders weren't all—'

'What?' Corman demanded, as the baker's voice petered out and he looked blank.

'That's right,' Lebeau encouraged, gently goading. 'Tell him all of it, Jessup.'

'Frank?' Corman demanded, genuinely puzzled. 'What is this? Weren't you hidden up with the rest?'

'I was hiding behind the top of cemetery hill,' Jessup admitted. 'But I had my field-glasses with me.'

'What did you see through them?'

'I saw a few of our boys riding with those Yankee cavalrymen.'

'I don't believe it!'

'Brad, I saw what I saw. Now don't you try to tell me different.'

'He saw what he saw,' Lebeau confirmed with a malicious glee. 'Tell him the rest. Do good by his warm Southern heart!'

'Landsakes, Lebeau!' the baker protested disgustedly. 'You recall Jack Mapes, Brad —him from just over the county line before the war?'

'Lieutenant Jack Mapes of our First

Texas Cavalry?' Corman inquired aghast. 'Are you telling me he was there? Your damned field-glasses are no good!'

'Them field-glasses of mine are real good!' Jessup declared indignantly. 'And Jacko Mapes was there. It ain't that far across from cemetery hill, Brad.'

'So my troop lieutenant has turned bandit,' Corman observed bitterly. 'Well, that doesn't surprise me too much. His behaviour to the civilian population up in Maryland was beyond the pale. I ought to have shot him myself!'

'Mapes isn't in command,' Lebeau advised. 'The rumour is he's running second to a Yankee major. Major Phileas Brock.'

'This is serious, Lebeau,' Corman said, noting that an oddly secretive grin glimmered in the saloonkeeper's eyes. 'It's far from a laughing matter.'

'It's no concern of ours,' Lebeau retorted. 'Just thought you ought to know how matters stand.'

'It concerns everybody,' Corman parried. 'I don't like you, mister, and you don't like me. So what? Bad men can't be allowed to run riot. If we have no law to turn to, we must do the law's job ourselves.'

'That's right smack against the law,' Jessup reminded.

'The law we don't have?' Corman asked severely. 'Come on, Frank! Where are you today?'

'What can we do, boy?' the baker protested, though not vehemently.

'As much or as little as Raftville is prepared to undertake,' Corman answered, feeling peculiarly sidetracked. 'I came along here looking for my wife. Where is she?' He raised his voice and gazed around him. 'Can anybody tell me where Anne Corman is?'

'They've got her,' a male voice said laconically. 'She was took by them raiders. Her and Vesta Milligan and Jean Coltrane. Them three was bawling their heads off as the horsemen rode 'em away.'

'Sorry, Brad,' Jessup said, almost as an afterthought. 'That's how it was. Saw it through my field-glasses, and heard it plain enough.'

'Aw, our Southern girls have got used to rape!' another speaker remarked callously. 'They'll get fed. What's going to happen to us? Them thieves have got most of our money and valuables. If you can't spend, you can't eat. Tell that to your kids!'

'Three women seized!' Corman exploded. 'Don't you care? Can't you think about anything but your belly, Sykes?'

'Sure,' the pasty Colin Sykes acknowledged, 'you've had had a hard war, Captain, and this is a bad day for you. But we've seen our share of hardship too, and you might as well get used to how it is for us.'

'You contemptible polecat!' Corman yelled, hardly able to credit what he had just heard. 'I'd never have believed any man of this town could utter such heartless words!'

'He talks good sense,' Lebeau said, his tones superior to the point of smugness. 'We have to put up with what's happening to us now. The Yankees have to be accepted as masters. The trick is to stay alive, Corman. You do that by keeping low and seizing what you can, regardless of other folk. Better days will—'

'One more word out of you, Lebeau,' Corman warned, beside himself with fury and unable to recognise the man he had become, 'and I'll hit you so hard you'll never wake up again!'

'You quit your braying, soldier!' countered the giant of a man who had earlier

21

indicated that he was somehow associated with the saloonkeeper. 'I do Mr Lebeau's fighting for him. My name's "Iron Mike" Magraw. You'd do well to shiver in your boots when you hear it!'

Corman scowled disdainfully.

'Have you got suicide in mind, Corman?' Lebeau inquired. '"Iron Mike" Magraw was the bare-knuckle champion of the West Coast back in the Eighteen-fifties. He's half killed men of twice your force!'

'That's the size of it,' Magraw acknowledged grimly, stepping over the two dead bodies on the ground before him and towering above the captain, anvil-jawed and battle-scarred, with the sun picking out blood-red strands in his mane of tawny hair. 'I want to hear you apologise to Mr Lebeau. I won't have my boss mouthed at—by a scarecrow!'

'You'll hear no apology from me, you big lummox!' Corman responded, still too enraged to feel the slightest fear of his barrel-chested foe. 'But I will hear one from you. You can't insult an officer in this uniform and get away it, even if the cloth is in rags. Apologise, Magraw.'

'And if I don't?' 'Iron Mike' chortled, pantomiming fear.

'I'll wash your mouth out for you!'

'Where?'

'There's a horse-trough yonder.'

'Pah!'

Perhaps rashly, Corman stepped right up to the big man and, going for him instantly, Magraw grabbed the captain at the belt and throat and threw him backwards. Corman staggered a pace or two, then his spurs locked. Over he went, sitting down hard on his posterior, and he held his place for a moment, glowering upwards as 'Iron Mike' slowly retreated and beckoned at him with both hands.

TWO

The invitation was too utterly provoking to be ignored or resisted. Corman shoved himself erect, then, fists clenched and held at the height of his breastbone, advanced on Magraw. The big man took up a professional boxing pose and, knees slightly bent, started circling to the right and feinting with his left. 'Here it comes, soldier!' he cautioned, essaying a big right but holding it back amidst his own booming laughter. 'See how easy it is? That would have been the finish of you!'

It could have been too. Corman was pretty sure that he would have ducked too late if Magraw had let fly, and he was immediately conscious that it was no good fighting a champion with a novice's technique. He was going to lose for sure if he did that. Outweighed by over a hundred pounds, he had only his lightness of foot and wiry strength to rely upon. The nearer this battle got to a knock-'em-down and drag-'em-out, the better would be his chance. 'Here goes!' he snarled, taunting in his turn; then threw himself at Magraw, burying his right fist wrist-deep in the giant's solar plexus.

Magraw folded visibly, his eyes popping. 'Why you miserable tadpole!' he gulped. 'I'll cripple you for—!'

Corman silenced his opponent with a smash to the mouth. Magraw spat and looked exasperated. He gathered himself to deliver a major blow—and plainly intended to trigger it this time, and the smaller man prepared to duck the punch when it came, confident now that his timing would prove correct; but what in fact Magraw did took him completely by surprise, for the giant butted at him through his guard and made contact brow on brow, and it seemed to Corman that a ball of red ochre exploded inside his head and his sight abruptly dimmed into fields of shadow as his perspectives distorted.

Once more he lurched to the rear, fighting for his senses now, and he knew that once he had lost his footing he would not be allowed to rise again, for the intimations of a brawl were now present and he would undoubtedly be kicked and trampled half to death once he was on his back; so, reeling to his right and fending himself off the ground with his hand on that side, he kept turning round the legs of the slower moving Magraw until his own head cleared a little and the mighty Irishman showed signs of dizziness.

Gathering his will, Corman straightened and flew at his opponent again. He landed two punches that carried all his power on the giant's chin. Magraw staggered, and the very force of Corman's actions seemed to clear his own brain still further. Spitting blood, the big man threw a right and missed. Seizing this advantage, Corman swung in over the top with a vicious left hook. That punch knocked the last trace of contempt off the Irishman's face. He stiffened visibly, and his expression warned that he would be fighting in total earnest from this moment on. Yet his resolution did him no good, for his co-ordination was impaired and his enemy had the rhythm.

Corman banged in a left, then a right, and did the same again as Magraw pawed ineffectively at the air. Every blow struck home on the chin with the full weight of its delivery and, strong as he unquestionably was, Magraw began to weaken. His tread grew shaky and his eyes spun. Now his nose and mouth wept redly and cuts appeared in the swelling around his temples. The impression was one of increasing ruin. Magraw started to retreat, unable to resist the sheer fury of the captain's attack any longer, and it ought to have ended there and then as Corman sought to deliver a knock-out punch; but then, quite abruptly, the captain's strength began to fade and he realized that the effect of the earlier clash of foreheads was now draining him heavily. His efforts to keep going became still more frantic, and he bored in as best he could, only too aware that, if his energy failed him completely, he could still lose this fight to the big Irishman.

Then Corman received help of an unexpected kind, for the backs of his opponent's legs made heavy contact with the nearer end of the horse-trough which the captain had designated as the one in which Magraw's mouth was to be washed out. Now, his lower limbs giving out, the Irishman sat down in the trough, water flying into the air on either side of him. He sat there, pinned by the woodwork and roaring his fury and discomfort. Then he struggled to get free, but for a long moment could not prise his large buttocks out of the tightly constricting trough. During that time, Corman went on hitting him, and it was in sheer desperation that he finally managed to get a firm grip on the sides of the trough to either hand and force himself upright, liquid gushing out of the seat of his trousers and pooling at his feet.

There he stood, mouthing—almost a figure of fun indeed—and he fended at the still punching captain like one outraged by an unwarranted assault. Yet there remained an underlying determination in him, and he let go with a right hand again, opening the road for Corman as before, and the

27

captain hit over the top of his foeman's extended arm and landed his blow on the side of Magraw's mouth. The punch was hard enough, yes, but its effect was far from devastating, and all the difference was made when the giant's right heel slipped on a stone and he skated forward into a fall that brought the back of his head into very heavy contact with the woodwork at the end of the trough from which he had just escaped. The violent meeting of timber and bone immediately achieved what Corman had so far been unable to achieve, and Magraw sprawled on to his back and shuddered into unconsciousness. It was clear from the look of him that he would not be causing any more trouble that day.

Corman put both hands over his face. He was too drained to take the smallest pleasure in his victory, and lurched away to his right and thudded to rest against the rails along the front of the Black Boot saloon's verandah. He felt a shudder pass through the entire structure, and found himself half blind as he took his palms away from his eyes. It was obvious now that he was even more hurt than he had supposed. Close to fainting, he had to fight for every breath, and might well have collapsed had he been left to go on supporting himself, but then a rather slight shoulder was forced under his right armpit and he felt an arm tightening across his back. 'Let me help you,' a girl's voice said.

'Obliged,' he muttered. 'Thanks.'

'This way. Easy now.'

The pressure of body on body was to Corman's left. He went with it, striving to keep his feet and holding off the dark. Never had he been tested more severely, but it wasn't far that he had to go, and he was soon aware of being taken indoors and led through homely smelling spaces to a bed, where he was lowered on to soft linen and allowed to relax. After that everything slipped away from him and he was at peace.

For what could have been an age, the captain knew nothing. Then, slowly, he became conscious of a world of dull colours and formless dreams. Fragments of thought came and went. There was little sense to any of it, yet he fought to find sense—and found panic and a muttering delirium instead. He heard a voice soothing at his ear, and took a sort of comfort from the sound—and there was perfume and the feel of hair upon his face, while raindrops streamed gently across glass and a night wind blew. He opened his eyes momentarily on to a room filled with lamplight, then he was gone again, and there was another space in the dark before he groaned and came round fully, things back into drawing once more and their true perspectives restored. Then a cloth filled with cold water came to rest upon his forehead, and he knew that his female helper was still with him, though standing to his rear and out of his line of vision. 'Who is that?' he inquired.

'Mary Forbes,' the female voice replied softly. 'I brought you here yesterday. Don't you remember?'

'I remember it,' he assured her with a ballooning tongue, recalling the yellow-haired girl who had been crouched sobbing against the front of the Black Boot saloon when he had first come down from his house into Raftville's stricken main street. 'I remember you, Mary—from yesterday and way back.'

'Of course you do. I was the town's tomboy.'

'It was your grandpa and grandma lying

dead out there, wasn't it?'

'I'm afraid so,' she sighed.

'What happened to—?'

'You should go back to sleep, Captain,' the girl cut in. 'You're a sick man.'

'I've got a god-damned headache,' Corman complained, 'but I'm fair-to-middling otherwise.'

'Swearing about it won't help,' Mary Forbes advised. 'Go back to sleep, there's a good man.'

Corman choked out a tiny laugh. It struck him as funny that the girl should be chiding him for bad language one moment and calling him a good man the next. But she had the right of it, of course; he still wasn't worth a light. But a fellow who wore a captain's insignia couldn't give in to himself like that. He had apparently slept longer now than he had slept at any time for many a year. He was awake, by heck—and he meant to stay awake. Life was about doing. Sleep was for those who had ceased to do. 'I'm all right,' he said firmly, raising fingers to his forehead as the wet cloth was removed from it and feeling at the lumps of flesh above his eyes which must be swollen to several times their normal size. 'Hell, I must look a sight!'

'You do,' Mary promised. 'You're lucky there's nothing broken.'

'Uh, huh. It was no friendly knock of the skull that man Magraw gave me.'

'Well, I can see you're not going to do what I want you to do.'

'Another time,' he said as sweetly as he could. 'There are things to be done. I can't believe this whole town has become as selfish and uncaring as that hound Colin Sykes made it sound.'

'No,' the girl agreed. 'There are still plenty of decent people in the place. My grandparents weren't the last good folks.'

'If only I could make that one better for you, Miss Forbes,' Corman sighed.

'It will never get better, Captain,' the girl said. 'That pain will never go away. But you have your own trouble too. A terrible thing has happened to your wife, and it can't be much less bad for you.'

'It's a facer,' he admitted; 'but done is done. The most I can do is try to get Anne back and punish the men who kidnapped her. I need help. The town has to form a posse. We must ride those raiders down and put an end to them. We are not the only people who've been hurt. Others must be aching too. If the majority of us stick

32

together, we can do anything that has to be done.'

'I agree with you, Captain,' Mary Forbes said resolutely. 'I'm with you from start to finish, and I'm going to speak up on the street for what you say.'

'Then the sooner you're out there the better,' Corman said bluntly. 'Please don't call me captain. To you I'm Brad.'

'All right. If you'll call me Mary. You always did before you went away to war.'

Corman smiled as the girl stepped round in front of him, perfectly rounded, with large blue-green eyes, a wide mouth, and a nose that lay between high cheekbones as exactly as any nose could. 'That's better. Well, Mary?'

'They have almost a day on us, Brad,' the girl reminded, 'and haste never achieved anything but less speed. We must eat and drink. I'll make some breakfast.' She frowned, shaking her head. 'I honestly don't think you're ready for any of it.'

'Get some breakfast,' he said. 'I'll go along with you that far. As for the haste, I've lived with a live cat in my guts for the last four years. Whatever comes now, I'll never know the difference.'

The girl left the bedroom. Corman, still

33

fully dressed beneath his coverlet, stretched himself out to the full and tried to will away the pains in his head left by his injury. He knew what needed doing, and was all impatience to be getting on with it, but fear and confusion—as with death and damage—were rife in Raftville, and he could not be certain that there was enough spirit left in the townsmen to mount up and strike a blow for themselves. It was a fraught situation and, in the aftermath of the war, he had to admit to himself that there were rights and wrongs in it beyond the obvious ones. The Yankees ruled now and, despite the high words of their generals and politicians, they might well come down hard on a community—however badly wronged—that rode down the trail and exacted its own justice. A Yankee could do no wrong in Yankee eyes, and the honest men of Columbia were a long way from the present doings of the veteran bluecoat soldiery who had fought southwards in their names. Again, God damn the Union!

After a few minutes Mary Forbes reappeared. She carried a large tray on which were boiled eggs, sliced ham, white bread, marmalade and coffee. Corman forced himself to eat a couple of eggs and drink some sweetened coffee, while the tired-looking Mary—whom he judged to have been watching over him all night—contented herself with some bread and marmalade. 'How exactly did your grandparents get shot down?' Corman finally asked, as the girl poured him more coffee.

'I wasn't here,' she explained a trifle defensively. 'Would that I had been. I was over at the Wiggs farm. You know it.'

Corman gave his chin a slight jerk. 'A mile or so north of town. Had you gone over for eggs or something?'

'No, Adah Wiggs had another baby about a month ago,' Mary continued. 'She hasn't been up to snuff ever since. I've been doing a bit for her in the house. I was still there when those robbers rode into town. Though I didn't know it at the time, of course.' She paused. 'It was the sound of shooting that brought me back. As I came in across the land I felt in my bones that something was terribly wrong.'

'It was wrong all right,' the captain acknowledged. 'I imagine the old people were already lying in the street before you got home.'

'I told you so,' she reminded, adding that she had later been told that one of the thieves had lifted her grandfather's poke. 'You know how tight he always was with money, Brad. It seems he just couldn't bear parting. As the story runs, he went raging up the street after the Yankee who had robbed him, and that bluecoated devil gunned him down. Grandma went after the killer, waving a stick and remonstrating, and that evil brute shot her too.' Mary's voice quavered. 'How can men be so—so cruel? The animals behave much better than human beings.'

'That's true,' Corman allowed. 'Even jungle beasts only kill when they're scared or hungry.'

'Yesterday, Brad, I was drawn to you because you were the only person thinking right,' Mary Forbes confessed, a defiance in her tones telling that she felt no penitence for her bold admission. 'We've got to catch those raiders. Jack Mapes and his scum too. Before they lay waste the countryside.'

'We?' the captain temporised. 'You don't really figure on getting mixed up in this personally?'

'What else?' the girl protested. 'Why

do you suppose I'm so ready to help you? She best serves others when first she serves herself. Right? I want revenge, Brad—good old fashioned revenge—for the murder of my grandparents. And I'll still go to church on Sunday.'

'An eye for an eye, eh?'

'And a tooth for a tooth.'

'This is a fine conversation!' Corman remarked sourly. 'I'd like to make you stop at home, but I can't prevent you from doing what you're determined to do. On your own head be it!'

'That's all right. Nobody is responsible for me but myself.'

'More glib words.'

'I thought I'd made it quite clear, Brad,' she replied adamantly. 'I'll do whatever I have to do, and say whatever I have to say.'

'Hell-and-dammit! Where will it all take us?' Corman flared.

'To some kind of end?' the girl queried.

'Okay,' he said, nodding. 'Let's go outside and see if we can gather a posse. Alone, this thing's beyond us. We must have folk riding at our sides.'

'Will you let me do the talking, Brad?'

'Why?'

'I'm a woman, they know me better, and they liked my grandparents.' Mary Forbes smiled bleakly. 'Nor do I rant and posture.'

'I do?'

'It could be mistaken for that, Captain.'

Corman eyed the girl a trifle angrily. She could be mocking him, but he supposed it was a case where the truth hurt. He did take on a bit, and folk didn't always like that. In lesser circumstances, he might have given her a piece of his mind—and denied her allegation—but he wanted only results here, and he wanted them quickly. If Mary Forbes could touch the collective conscience better than he, so be it. 'Have it your way,' he said curtly. 'Anyhow, I want to go up to my house and fetch my horse. I left the poor brute tied there when I came down into the street.'

The girl set the breakfast tray aside, then headed for the door. Corman got off the bed while she was doing this and, fighting off a moment of vertigo, had an important afterthought. 'Mary.'

Pausing, she looked across her shoulder. 'Yes?'

'Have you got a pistol in the house?' he requested. 'All us Southern boys were disarmed at the surrender. I must have a weapon.'

'There's grandfather's pistol,' Mary said. 'I suppose you can have that. He won't be asking for it again.'

'Fetch it,' Corman urged.

The girl walked out of the room. She turned right, and Corman soon heard her pass through another door—into what had been her grandfather's sleeping place, he imagined—and she returned within the minute holding an almost new Navy Colt in her hand. 'Will this do?'

'You bet it will!' he declared. 'There's no better pistol than this.'

Mary handed him the weapon, and two spare cylinders to go with it. He checked the revolver for its loads, found them good, then did the same with the cylinders, nodding his satisfaction over them too. After that he thrust the gun into his Army holster and pocketed the cylinders.

Leaving the room in the girl's wake, Corman followed her through the hall and out into the street, where he stopped and looked around him while she went on about the business that she had requested for herself. The captain saw at once that yesterday's attempt by the raiders to burn the town must have been a rather perfunctory effort, for no more than a third of the properties had been seriously damaged by the fires and many of the buildings—including the Forbes house—were completely intact and no more than blistered or discoloured by the heat and smoke. He guessed the renegades, like most guilty men, had been in a hurry to leave the scene of their crimes, and they had been content just to take the town's valuables and the three women with them. Sighing to himself, Corman felt some relief, for the rebuilding in Raftville would be nothing like total, and that meant most of the men would be able to think of other matters than putting roofs over the heads of their families.

Corman faced left. He walked along the main street and up the slope beyond. Approaching his home, he saw his horse standing at the picket fence much as he had left it. Breaking the stallion's tie, he gave the brute a consolatory slap on the rump and swung into his saddle, riding slowly back down the ground up which he had just come on foot and studying what human activity he could see out-of-doors with a calculating eye. The day was still young and little energy was being manifested as yet. A feeling of apathy and defeat still reigned, and there was nothing to suggest that Mary Forbes was proving any kind of inspiration among her friends. Altogether, his brain numb—and joints plagued by stiffness—he was not at his most sanguine and, when he reached Mary's house again, he dismounted and bowed his head against his saddle, bracing himself for the disappointment which he feared the girl's reappearance would bring. If she failed, his plans would fail with her; and he had no clear idea of what he was going to do beyond that. Get drunk, he wouldn't wonder! It was many a long year since he had last done that.

Another quarter of an hour went by. Corman remained bent to his saddle, trying to shake off his feelings of illness and gloom. Then, as he heard a light footfall at his back, a hand came to rest on his shoulder and, turning, he found himself looking down into Mary's face. 'Well,' he asked, attempting grim humour, 'how many heroes do we have?'

'It isn't that bad!' the girl protested. 'Frank Jessup has been doing some talking of his own. I figure we've put together a party of eight or more. No army, I do agree, but—'

'More than I expected,' Corman admitted, though his spirits were not greatly raised. 'Enough at a pinch.'

'Frank thinks so,' Mary said. 'He's of the opinion that too many cooks spoil the broth.'

'I've seen it myself,' the captain conceded. 'I wonder if Frank has any idea of what direction those renegades went in when they left here?'

'He hasn't. I did ask him. There was rain last night, Brad. It will have washed out any sign.'

'We can't afford to ride too many wasted miles,' Corman observed. 'I wonder if anybody has a clear notion.'

Mary snapped her fingers and looked momentarily excited. 'Lebeau! Of course, I remember now!'

'What do you remember, Mary?'

'It was as I was nearing town,' she explained, when I was running back across the land from Wiggs' farm. I glanced towards the western end of town, and saw Rufus Lebeau there. He was encircled by the raiders, and the Yankee officer was talking to him.'

'Odd,' Corman mused. 'Why wasn't he tight in his bolt-hole—with other folk getting shot I mean? He was their prisoner? I don't trust that varmint. Especially the way he was talking before "Iron Mike" made to set about me.'

'I suppose he was a prisoner,' Mary said. 'It looked like it. You mustn't read too much into things. All I meant was: Rufus was close by as those raiders rode off and should have a good idea of the direction they took. It has to be promising.'

'Granted,' Corman said thoughtfully. 'I must have a word with Rufus, and right now.'

'After what you did to Mike Magraw?' Mary wondered aghast.

'That was yesterday,' the captain commented. 'These things happen among men, Mary. I don't aim to kick up any fuss with Lebeau today. If there's further trouble, it'll have to be him who starts it.'

'I'm not easy about it.'

'I need to hear what he has to say.'

'Very well,' the girl breathed. 'I suppose it has to be so.'

'Right. Then I'm going along to the Black Boot. I expect he'll be there.'

Mary nodded.

'You get your horse out,' Corman advised, 'then put together some supplies.'

'I'll do that, Brad.'

Straightening away from his saddle, Corman squared his shoulders and headed down the street towards the Black Boot saloon.

THREE

It took Corman less than a minute to reach the Black Boot. After crossing the saloon's verandah, he checked and peered into the bar-room across the top of the batwings. He could see a few signs of fire-damage on the left of the room, but the place appeared perfectly habitable and he could make out the figures of men present through the inner gloom. He didn't feel too brave about what he had to do, but knew he must not let any trace of apprehension show, so he pushed open the swing-doors and stepped inside, moving jauntily over the floorboards as his gaze sought the man he had come to see.

Rufus Lebeau was indeed present. He

44

stood at the bar and was staring into the figured glass at the back of it. 'Iron Mike' Magraw stood at Lebeau's left shoulder, his elbow on the divide and his gaze travelling in the same direction as the saloonkeeper's, with the difference that he could hardly see out of his grossly swollen eyes and was snuffling audibly as he tried to breathe through his cut and flattened nostrils. There were other men present too, at the tables for the most part, and the air was thick with tobacco smoke and reeked of spirits and the cheap perfumes of the whores who paraded in their petticoats along the balcony high up at the rear of the big room.

Little notice was taken of Corman as he traversed the floor—though he sensed that everybody was in fact acutely sensitive to his presence—and he had to get right up to the divide and close enough to perceive the fine stubble left at the corners of the saloonkeeper's recently shaven jaw before Lebeau acknowledged his visit with an upraised finger and said: 'You've a nerve, Corman.'

'A good one,' the captain agreed easily. 'How are you?'

'Nigh enough, Rufus.'

'What have you been doing with young Mary?'

'Nothing I shouldn't.'

'You're a damned liar!' Lebeau scorned. 'I say you've been up to plenty you shouldn't.'

'Explain that,' Corman, 'and do a good job of it. I'm not in the mood for too much of your old buck, sir!'

'Have a drink?'

'Thank you, no,' the captain responded. 'Well?'

'We've just heard a rumour in here that that fool of a girl has been in several houses along the street and drumming up a posse. Talking for you, I'd say. Great balls of fire, Corman! You've had four years of war! Are you that greedy for blood? I suppose you've seen all your followers killed, and now you've come home to get the same job done here. Let it lie, man! Leave it alone! Those soldiers didn't do us that much harm. We've had a few properties destroyed, some valuables stolen, and three pretty women abducted. Yes, yes, I know one of them is your wife, but it should be something you're prepared to put up with. Is any part of what's happened worth seeing a pack of fools shot out of their

46

saddles for? It can't be!'

'I say it is!' Corman retorted. 'We already know what Quantrell and "Bloody Bill" Anderson are capable of. The bunch that rode through here will soon be just as bad. They must be stopped before they really get the blood lust. I'm telling you, Rufus—it is up to us!'

'Don't stick your nose in!' Lebeau persisted. 'It's a problem for the Federals. Let the boys in blue get round to it. Failing that, leave it to a town with better resources to tackle the job. There's no imperative, Corman!'

'Yes, you can trot it out in a gentleman's words when you're of the mind,' the captain conceded. 'So can I, sir. But I prefer the straight talk of a straight man. You're afraid, Lebeau. I can feel it!'

'W-what?' the saloonkeeper spluttered.

'You're a coward, Rufus—that's what's up with you!' Corman declared, the possibility that had been festering in his mind ever since he had left Mary Forbes suddenly showing its ugly core. 'If that's all of it.'

'Meaning what?'

'I don't know. You were seen hob-nobbing with the renegades.'

47

Lebeau blinked. He had clearly been startled, and what could have been a shadow of fear touched his features. 'Hobnobbing, be damned!' he roared, casting a meaningful glance towards a rat-faced man whose head was hung in braids of straw-coloured hair. This fellow, who sported a tied-down pistol—a new thing among men who were handy with guns—sat alone and expressionless at a table near the centre of the room. 'Johnny!'

'I hear you, boss,' the rat-faced Johnny said, rolling on to his left buttock to bring his holster into the best position for a quick grab. 'Wasn't I close by? This one's a rattlesnake, and he's rattling at you. I reckon he needs his head blown off.'

'There's an accusation in it somewhere,' Lebeau fumed. 'Tell him what I was there for, Johnny.'

'You were pleadin' for them bitches, boss,' said the man with the braided head, his small blue eyes full of ice and dawning hatred.

'Yes, I was pleading for those girls,' Lebeau agreed, sounding almost tearful in his outraged self-righteousness. 'I pleaded for them as hard as I knew how. Johnny,

48

I might have got myself shot if I'd gone on a moment longer. Isn't that true?'

'As steel, boss,' the rat-faced man confirmed emphatically. 'Be careful, soldier. If you doubt the word of Rufus Lebeau, you also doubt the word of Johnny Hiker, and there are graves between here and the Gulf that testify to how dangerous that is.'

Corman was unafraid, and let Hiker see it. But he had pushed this far enough, and felt that he was marginally in the wrong. He had said that he wouldn't start trouble, yet here he was at the edge of a potentially lethal exchange; and, worse still, this when he required what could be regarded as a favour of Lebeau. After all, there was no proof of anything against the man and he could be entirely innocent of all wrong-doing. If veiled, he had better offer an apology—or at least be conciliatory. At best, he was going to come out of this with nothing if he didn't, and that would make a waste of his walk to the saloon. 'There may have been a misunderstanding here, Rufus. The one important fact is that you were the last man to see those renegades when they were leaving the town. Can you say with certainty in which direction they were travelling?'

A grim little chuckle sounded deep in Lebeau's throat. 'Yes, you'd better watch your tongue, Corman. But I don't want trouble any more than you now seem to. So I'm going to tell you first about Johnny Hiker. He's the Fort Worth pistolero—the best gun there is. Just think what could have happened to you.'

'You seem to have champions all over the place, Lebeau,' Corman said drily, sliding a covertly amused glance at "Iron Mike" Magraw, who had just decided to look fixedly in the opposite direction. 'They must cost you more than they're worth.'

'None of your business!'

'But the other matter is. Will you help?'

'Why should I help you bring more grief to Raftville?'

'It's all a question of putting right what we can, then doing our best to save others.'

'I don't find that a convincing argument,' Lebeau said flatly. 'These are days when we have to look out for the main chance, and hang others. I ask you again to leave it alone.'

'This is not going to harm or cost you in any way,' Corman returned. 'All you have to do is supply what you know, then forget about it.'

'Aw, he's going to pester the life out of you, Mr Lebeau,' Johnny Hiker said disdainfully. 'Maybe you should tell him what he wants, and let him get the hell out of here.'

'You're right, Johnny,' Lebeau said indifferently—'you're right. What he and others in this town do is no skin off our backs. Let them get themselves killed! It's a big country out there, and a posse from Raftville can be swallowed up as readily as any other.' He considered the brightly polished toes of his boots, while stroking his portly middle. 'I heard the Yankee major speak of Nacona. He and the men with him rode off northwards.'

'Nacona,' Corman reflected. 'That's right up on the Red river—empty country for the most part, farms and cattleland. Not many rich pickings there.'

'Not so many Union patrols either,' Lebeau reminded. 'You can only ride so far and mop up so much.'

Frowning, Corman nodded slowly. As a veteran cavalryman himself, he understood what had just been said. It was wiser to take a little less in safety than to go for a bit more at considerable risk. Yet, knowing his fellow men—and the greedier ones in particular—he judged that a band of desperadoes, bent on quick pickings, would be willing to risk capture and death while crossing richer and more populous land in pursuit of the swifter fortune. When he came to examine it closely, he realized that he would have banked on the renegades turning off to the left on leaving Raftville and heading south towards Dallas and Fort Worth; but he could be sure of nothing. He had sought information of Rufus Lebeau and been given it. The saloonkeeper had been sneering in his delivery, but there had been no intimations of duplicity present, so he, Corman, was more or less obligated to believe what he had been told. His head came up. 'Okay—thanks,' he said; and then he turned on his heel and made for the swing-doors.

'Good luck!' Lebeau called at his back; and Johnny Hiker put in a snigger.

Corman ignored them both. He shouldered on to the verandah outside. Then he stepped down into the street and strode back to Mary Forbes's house. The girl was now standing with horse in hand, and she had a number of mounted men clustered near her. Corman felt a vague sense of pleasure and relief. It had all been done for him. Mary Forbes seemed to have performed a sort of magic. She had achieved for him a piece of organisation that he had feared might prove rather difficult. There had been no pain to himself, and he was grateful. 'Well done, Mary,' he said.

'We shall be nine,' she said, smiling. 'There's Bill Tidy—you'll remember him —and Joe Sawyer and Tony Sales have also decided to ride with us.'

Corman shared a single nod all round. The folk present all knew each other well enough and seemed to feel that introductions and effusive greetings were unnecessary. If there was anybody here that he hadn't met before, he guessed he'd get to know them on the trail. Frank Jessup was there sure enough, and he was the man who mattered most. They touched hats to each other.

'Do we go?' Mary Forbes asked, mounting up.

Corman stepped into his own saddle. 'Right now,' he replied, and prodded his horse out to the party's head.

They trotted their way beyond Raftville's limits, and then Frank Jessup surged up to the captain's left shoulder and asked: 'Where away, boy?'

'Yes,' Mary put in from the other side, 'did you get anything out of Rufus Lebeau?'

Corman hesitated. Contradictory currents of thought were still sweeping his mind.

'These people have the right to know,' Mary prompted.

The captain smiled wryly at his pommel. Yes, these folk did have the right to know. They were volunteers, and this wasn't the army. He wouldn't be captain-absolute on this ride. Those days were in the past. 'I had a short talk with Lebeau, Mary. He told me he heard the Yankee major say that the renegades were bound for Nacona.'

'The river country,' Jessup mused. 'So we'll be riding north. I figured on the other direction—south.'

'So did I,' Corman said. 'Toward Bowie.' He passed a hand across his mouth. 'You put off, Frank?'

'It doesn't sit right, that's all.'

'It doesn't with me either,' the captain

admitted. 'But Lebeau must know what he heard.'

'I vow he shouldn't have heard it,' Jessup growled. 'Was it fed him?'

'Wouldn't think so,' Corman said, though the doubt was strong in him now. If a trustworthy instinct like Jessup's found cause to wonder, then the cause must be there. The logic of the matter did indeed fight shy of close examination. Honestly speaking, anybody with a grain of sense must feel the same about it. Yet the need for trust remained. 'Rufus was sure.'

'He's no good, Brad,' Jessup chewed.

'Tell me not in mournful numbers!' Corman pleaded, spurring his horse to a canter and moving ahead of the baker and the girl.

The captain was left to himself after that, and the posse entered a more undulating country about five miles beyond Raftville. Here grassy rises broke the horizon's purple lines and buttermilk skies turned hazily blue as the morning sun gathered power and shone brightly behind the thinning cloud layers of the middle heavens. Now a wedge of green country came thrusting at the party, its presence forming a natural division of the paths that had served generations of travellers on this part of the prairie. Indecisive still, Corman gazed intently at the parting of the ways and finally made up his mind that he would be betraying both his companions and himself if he didn't take the chance to put his nagging doubts to rest once and for all; so, lifting his right hand to check the posse, he wheeled his horse about and called: 'I'm going to take a ride down the southern fork of the trail. You're all plenty smart enough to guess why, so I won't go into it further. Frank, you take over. Keep heading towards the Red river. I'll ride round the back of the land and meet up with you again later in the day. Sooner—and by a shorter route—if I spot anything.'

'Away you go!' Jessup prompted.

Corman rode off at speed. The great wedge of earth soon loomed above him. He rounded its sharp end and began making for the sun. Then, slowing, he put his eyes to the ground and concentrated, seeking any trace which might suggest that the renegades had yesterday ridden over the trail which led southwards, but the grass and soil were still damp with last night's rain and nothing suspicious was discernible. He maintained his attention for twenty minutes or more, but was constantly jarred by the hooves beneath him as they made rhythmic contact with the hard centre of the beaten track. His head began to ache badly again, and he decided that, for good or ill, he had better give up this folly now; but he was getting ready to turn aside, when his interest was quickened once more by the presence of a cast horeseshoe on the trail before him.

Coming to the hoof-iron, Corman reined in and stepped down. Crouching, he picked the cast shoe up and peered at it closely. Debris of this kind was of course common in this day of the rider, and one thrown iron was much like another, but this one was new enough to have the look of an army farrier about its bevelling and, what was more important, still had hoof tissue attached to its clinched nails. A man of great experience in these matters, Corman judged that the shoe had been cast less through the repetitive damage of travel than the rottenness of actual disease. The hoof had softened and split, and the shoe had kicked away, thus leaving somebody with a mount that was no longer much good to him. Yes, everything was right; it could easily be a soldier.

Corman threw the cast horseshoe aside. Then he remounted and nudged his horse back into motion. For all his moment of elation, the captain realized that his find might mean much less than he hoped. The bevelling didn't really count for a lot—since plenty of civilian blacksmiths were a mite fancy too—but if the misfortune of the thrown shoe had occurred to a soldier, in transit with other riders of his own kind, there was a strong probability that the denuded animal would have been destroyed at the trailside once its total incapacity had been accepted. Thus, if the horse had belonged to one of the renegades, headed south after all, there was the chance that he would come upon its remains before long. If that should happen, much of the greatest importance would have been proved.

The captain rode on for a few minutes longer, and the trail started settling towards a stream flanked with willows and cottonwoods. The sheen of spring was on the greenery, and Corman's eyes were drawn to the first marigolds and marsh lilies budding beneath it. Suddenly there was much ado in a thicket, where nesting birds fluttered and shrilled in an outburst of alarmed activity, but Corman paid this disturbance little attention, for his gaze was snatched back in the opposite direction as the shadow of a drifting buzzard brushed the ground to the right and on this side of the ford directly ahead of him.

Lifting in his stirrups, he made out a shape lying in the grass above which the hawk swept. Excitement magnetised his spine, and he slapped his mount towards the water, halting it just short of the ford and springing down again. He'd got it right, by Jupiter! There was a dead horse lying near the waterside, and he could already see that it had been shot through the head. Yet, as he closed in to inspect the carcase—his eyes taking in every detail—he could see nothing which told him anything about the defunct creature's ownership. What he needed was the confirmation that Lebeau had deliberately deceived him as to the direction in which the renegades had travelled away from Raftville. Then, as he walked around the dead beast's haunches, he saw the brand of the U.S Army burned into the smoky hide there and his last doubt left him. This had been a cavalry horse for sure, and it was ninety-nine point nine percent certain that it had belonged to one of the renegades who had robbed and burned in Raftville just over a day ago.

Standing over the remains, Corman was savouring his dubious success—and putting his mind to future courses—when a shot rang out and a bullet tore at the collar of his coat, causing particles of cloth to flutter and his flesh to shrink from the nearest of near misses.

FOUR

Corman's battle-quickened reflexes were still with him. He dropped instantly behind the carcase of the dead horse, drawing his revolver as he hit the ground and a second slug rushed through the air that he had just vacated. Wriggling in close to the lifeless mount's spine, he cocked his pistol and raised his head sufficiently to look over the equine ribs that formed his cover and a succession of shots greeted this latest movement. The bullets were all well aimed and drove deep into the putrefying flesh of the extinct gelding's barrel, and Corman was content to keep low and let the fusillade blow itself out, aware now that the man trying to kill him was shooting from the clumped greenery where the nesting birds had created such a disturbance only a minute or two ago. He couldn't think where his mind had been; the warning was plain enough. It was simply that he had had no good reason to expect foul play.

The captain began to count under his breath. He slowly raised his head again on reaching ten. There was another bang, and a further tiny missile sang inches above his crown. But this time he thrust out the Navy Colt which Mary Forbes had given him and blazed at the spot where he believed the bushwhacker to be concealed. He saw a twig and some new leaves jump away from their parent growth, and a cry of pain reached his ears in the same moment. Corman felt a bitter satisfaction. Nicely done. Not only had he correctly guessed his enemy's position, but he had also shot straight. He could finish the bushwhacker now. So he rose to his knees and triggered off the remaining five shots in his cylinder at high speed, the slugs all tearing into the same circle of growth at which he aimed them, thus creating more ruin where the spring had produced so much beauty. Then, quickly swapping his spent magazine for a fresh one from his pocket, he levered the new cylinder into place and locked it in, thumbing back his hammer again and pausing against a possible reaction from the greenery. None came, and Corman was convinced that his enemy had indeed received his quietus and could now be approached with safety; but the captain had yet to leave cover, when he made out a man's figure creeping backwards through the waterside growth and cursed himself for new thoughtlessness as he realized that his first bullet must have done no more than wing the bushwhacker, and that the other must have flattened under his subsequent blaze of shots and now be in a fair way to escaping.

Considering the width of ground between him and the withdrawing gunman, Corman judged it too big a space to risk crossing on foot. The bushwhacker might have no stomach for a gun battle, but it was unlikely that he would pass up the opportunity for a clear shot. The wild dash could prove suicidal. Yet the captain perceived that, whatever he did, risk there had to be—if he were not to simply hold off and let the bushwhacker get away with attempted murder—and he calculated that his best chance of downing the would-be killer would be from horseback. So he sprang over the dead horse before him and ran to his own animal, climbing astride it and gathering up his reins. Then he put spurs to hide, and was just beginning to lunge forward, when the waterside gun banged again and he saw blood appear as lead nicked his mount's left shoulder. Hurt, the creature reared steeply and let out a furious neighing, and it unshipped its rider with some violence and sent him flying backwards over his cantle.

Corman struck the ground hard, and he felt his senses dip and whirl, but he hung on to consciousness and forced himself upright again, throwing out his right arm and aiming once more at the little he could see of the retreating bushwhacker. He fired, aware that his chances of making another hit were slight, and this was how it turned out, for the gunman vanished completely from his view and the noise of his withdrawal through the greenery became less pronounced by the second. He was indeed already more than a hundred yards beyond the captain's position and virtually safe, since he was unlikely to have left his horse too far away.

But Corman could not let it end that tamely. Sucking a deep breath, he hurled himself into a run towards the waterside area in which he deemed his man to be, legging it now as he had not done in many a year, and he almost flew over the grass, lurching and staggering somewhat where the ground was tussocky, and his charge took him finally to the edge of a place where the stream turned sharply to the right and the ground on the left of the water became a slope strewn with thorn bushes and boulders and had a stand of aspens on top.

Lungs almost bursting now, the captain saw that his enemy had already left the waterside greenery and was heading uphill to the left in a sprinting climb. Crouched, the man was still no real target, and Corman shot at him once only—more in frustration than anything else—and the bushwhacker blasted back at him in much the same spirit, showing his rat-face for an instant and the braided hair bobbing at his nape.

Johnny Hiker! Corman was prepared to

swear that his would-be murderer was Johnny Hiker, Rufus Lebeau's champion gun! 'Stand and fight, you damned coward!' the captain croaked at the bushwhacker's receding shape; but the other ignored him and then disappeared into the trees atop that slope, and Corman jerked to a halt, knowing that he was physically incapable of catching his enemy in his present state of distress. He had taken too much out of himself at the beginning of his dash, and no man in his middle thirties could afford to do that. He would have to wait for another time and place to settle his score with Johnny Hiker—and Rufus Lebeau, the scheming master who had undoubtedly set the bushwhacker on.

Corman put up his revolver. Then he faced about and picked a path back to his horse. The beast had turned aside and travelled only yards after being hurt, and it was now standing in a state of shock, its nose almost touching the ground and sweat oozing from its puckering flanks. Lifting the mount's head up again, Corman examined the wound on the brute's shoulder, but the hurt was as superficial as he had at first imagined and should not reduce the creature's performance by very much.

Wishing to do what he could for the animal, the captain led the horse down to the ford, where he laved its wound and let it drink. After that—and several minutes' rest—he drew the mount back on to the trail and turned its head northwards. Then, swinging up, he started riding back over the ground that he had covered during his investigative journey southwards—having decided that it would be quicker to catch up with his posse this way than by galloping a big curve around the back of the land as he had originally intended—and he soon regained the wedge of country where he had left his companions and rode on northwards for a few hours thereafter, coming up with the party now under Frank Jessup's leadership towards the end of the afternoon.

Answering the general greeting with a wave of his hand, Corman fell in at Jessup's side and started telling the baker all that had happened to him since they had parted company during the morning.

Jessup brought the posse to a bunched halt and heard him out, then said: 'You know what you've been telling us, Brad. You've been telling us that Rufus Lebeau is involved somehow with that Yankee

66

major and his robbers—which is sorta what we feared. You certain it was Johnny Hiker who tried to drygulch you, boy?'

'It was him all right,' Corman replied. 'I saw him clear enough to take my affy on that. If you stop to think about it, who the devil else would have wanted to shoot a gun at me? I remember you saying that Lebeau spread a kind of panic at Raftville before those renegades struck. It was a real good method of protecting that bunch.'

'Crafty as all-get-out,' Jessup commented, 'but it sure does read right.'

'It happened, whatever it was,' Mary Forbes interrupted impatiently. 'Are you going to chew it over until there's nothing left? And men say women are the talkers!'

Corman pulled a jib at the girl's accusing bluntness. 'It's far from being that bad!' he protested. 'I told Frank everything as fast as I could, and I had to get it right. Yes, Mary. I've heard you. All have a right to their say. Does anybody else want to put a word in? What about you, Bill?'

Bill Tidy rasped the stubble on his shrunken, scaly jaw, a turkey gobble in his shrunken throat and a bead of moisture running from a collapsed nostril. 'There's evidence all right,' he averred huskily, shifting a chaw from one side of his mouth to the other and revealing the gapped yellow teeth in his blue gums. 'So south's our road then? You don't aim to take us back all the way we've ridden today, Brad?'

'No need for that,' Corman said, noting that the nearby Joe Sawyer had winked an eye and turned a pitying face to heaven. 'We'll swing back south through west from here, Bill—over the route that I'd planned to catch up with you people if things had stood so that I started from further down country than was the case. We'll aim for the town of Bowie.'

'You see that as the next target for them bad guys, Cap'n?' inquired a fellow named Luther Kiln, the level of his head topping Corman's by several inches as they both sat tall in their saddles and adjacent.

'I've favoured it all along,' the captain said, 'and it was the next place down the trail from where I got fired on. I'm ready to gamble on it, Luther.'

'Reckon that satisfies me, Cap'n,' Kiln said. 'How about you, young Mary?'

'It seems a reasonable risk to me,' the girl admitted. 'We have lost a whole day whatever we do.'

'We're far more sure of what we're doing now,' Corman reminded, 'so we can perhaps remedy it. Anybody else want to say anything?'

Faces swivelled. There was a shaking of heads and a shrugging of shoulders. Corman regarded it as settled. Leaving the trail, he spurred off westwards, and the others sorted themselves out a little raggedly and followed him as order emerged. And thus, spread upon the grass, the riders galloped onwards, turning into the south as the captain showed the way, and before long they were far out on untracked prairie and heading for Bowie.

Corman would have liked to let his mind rest, but the lack of any real shape or certainty in things forced him to keep thinking ahead. He decided that he would ask his companions to spend the night well outside Bowie, while he went into town—apparently as an ordinary rider—to discover whether or not the renegades had attacked the place that day. If they hadn't, it was likely that they would do so tomorrow—which would require him to have some counter activity provisionally thought out—but that planning could wait until he was sure that it was really needed, since he could not ignore the possibility that even now he had read this business all wrong and Phileas Brock's next depredations would come elsewhere. If that should turn out to be the way of it, in defiance of his logic and reason, he would just have to wipe his mental slate clean and begin again, using Bowie as his starting point, but all that would depend upon a whole new intake of information that he could not even guess at for the moment.

Apart from a single stop for rest, the ride went on without pause and the day faded with it. By dusk the mounts had been reduced to little more than a tired trot, but Corman judged that his posse was now within three or four miles of Bowie and that it was time for his friends to eat and bed down. So he told them that, and the other things he had in mind, inviting comment, but, as he had expected, receiving none from Mary Forbes and the worn out men from Raftville, since it was clearly impossible to do much more than he suggested where Bowie was concerned. Nodding at their tacit acceptance of his intentions, he pointed out to them a deep fold in the prairie, where he considered a night's safe sleep should be possible, and, after he had seen them dip beneath the land, he stirred his horse and rode onwards in the direction of Bowie.

Guessing a little as to his exact position upon the land, Corman needed a slice of luck to find the last part of his way into Bowie and was fortunate enough to cut the town trail about a quarter of an hour later in sight of the clustered lights which marked the position of the place to his right. Turning, he began riding down a shallow incline and soon entered the built-up area, where he reduced his horse to the slowest of walks and absorbed the peace of the main street, at once certain that nothing seriously untoward had occurred in Bowie during the last day.

Pleased for the town, but made more uncertain in himself by the fact of it, Corman was preparing to let his sense of anticlimax govern his next action and turn his horse about—when he heard a plaintive song issuing from a nearby saloon. A lover of music—who had heard little in a long time—he was seduced by the melody and words of *In the Hills of Old Virginia* and decided that a few minutes spent in the drinking place would do nobody any harm;

so he sent his mount nosing up to the saloon's hitching rail and swung down, tying the animal and then stepping up to the batwings.

He entered the bar-room, where the lighting was shadowy and inadequate. The singer, female and past her best, held the centre of the stage at the back of the room, and she glanced at him with what he recognised as the interest of habit as he glanced at her faded silks and old feathers. The woman's voice no longer sounded quite as haunting as it had from the street, but she was nevertheless worth listening to, and he smiled appreciation as he made for the bar and ordered a mug of light beer from the gross, cross-eyed keeper yawning there in the absence of any substantial trade; and he had put his money down and was about to pick up his drink, when a male voice that was thick with the Irish brogue called: 'By the saints and all the holy relics! If it ain't the captain himself! Now what unlikely corner of hell did you come smoking up from, Mr Corman?'

The captain looked quickly to his left. He saw there, bellied up to the divide, a very large and muscular man whose presence he had somehow missed before. The other wore the uniform of a sergeant-major in the Confederate cavalry and was peering at him over a black and unlighted corncob pipe with what could only be described as pure delight. 'Gilhooley!' Corman responded wryly, for where the big man was trouble was usually lurking. 'Haven't they hanged you yet?'

'No, Captain,' the sergeant-major returned smugly, the piggy eyes under his bushy brows full of mischievous humour. 'I've bought up all the rope!'

'That'd do it,' Corman acknowledged. 'Well, how are you? I'd forgotten this town was your home.'

'And there was me hopin' it was on account of my good self you had appeared in this den of iniquity,' Gilhooley sighed, pretending disappointment.

'Fat chance, Sergeant-major!' Corman scorned. 'I see you got home ahead of me. But that would be natural enough. I guess they pulled you out after Spotsylvania. I wasn't sure if you and the rest were dead or alive. I got seconded to Johnston's staff, and ended up as a Texas representative with General Lee at the surrender. Short commons, eh?'

'I guess the general did what he could for us.'

'He did that,' Corman said fervently. 'We'd all known for weeks that it was over. Thank God Grant was in the mood to be generous. It could have been a lot worse.'

'Cryin' shame, Captain—when you look back—all of it.'

'Assuredly,' Corman agreed. 'All those mothers' sons—and for what?' He shook his head, then swallowed some beer. 'I suppose it was a nice piece of history to have lived through. "A war like no other yet"—that's how an English war correspondent described it. He said our methods of waging the fight made recent battles in Europe look old fashioned.'

'Sure and the world moves on,' Gilhooley commented inconsequentially. 'I'd offer you a drink, but we're still in uniform, and I must defer to rank.'

'Let's drop that nonsense, Hank!' Corman advised, chuckling. 'I'm just Brad Corman now—of Raftville—and that's no different from being Hank Gilhooley of this town. Whisky?'

'I'd never shame the shamrock!' Gilhooley declared. 'I'll have a shot o' rye

74

with you, Mr Corman.'

The captain jerked his chin at the barman, and pointed at Gilhooley's glass. He rolled another coin on the divide as the spirit was poured.

'To us, Captain!' Gilhooley toasted. 'Can't say as I know any better men.'

'To us,' Corman echoed.

Putting his glass down, Gilhooley sleeved off his lips. 'So what are you doing in Bowie at this hour of the day?' the big Irishman inquired conversationally.

'There you put me on the spot, Hank,' the captain returned hestitantly. 'I'm looking for some men.'

'Guys to work for you maybe?'

Corman shook his head strongly. He wanted to keep this truthful, but wasn't sure how much it would be wise to tell the Irishman about his mission. Though it was already clear to him that somebody in Bowie ought to be made aware of the perhaps imminent threat to the town from the mixed renegade soldiery. Weighing his words now, he said: 'I got home yesterday and found that Raftville had just been raided by renegade soldiery. A mixed bunch, if you'd believe it. Yankees and a few of our boys. There's a Union major named Brock in charge, and he's got our Lieutenant Jack Mapes in tow. Now mind me, Hank. That murderous bunch could be preparing to raid this town tomorrow or some time soon. I'm not altogether sure about it, but you must stay watchful.'

Gilhooley whistled softly to himself. 'Be Jasus! There's been some talk of a new style banditry, and that's a fact. You've spoiled my drinking time, Captain, but it's better to be told.'

'I think so,' Corman said.

'Did they rob your town bare?'

'Enough. They took my wife.'

'That ain't on the bill,' Gilhooley gritted. 'That's a gallows job.'

'Two other girls were abducted as well.'

'Rape I never could abide.'

'That's the shameful word for it, Hank,' Corman acknowledged.

'What can I do, Mr Corman? Do you have need of a strong arm?'

'Bowie may have the greater need,' Corman reminded. 'There's no law in Texas but what we make for ourselves now. If those renegades show up here, Bowie will need a man like you to help marshal it.'

'Maybe. But—'

76

'But me no buts, Hank,' the captain said decisively. 'This is my fight as yet; but only God knows who I may be glad to call on for help before it's all over.'

'Well, you know where I am,' Gilhooley said. 'If you need me, just holler.'

'Thank you.'

Gilhooley inclined his head. 'Are you staying in town tonight? There's a bed you can have at my house.'

'No. I'll be leaving shortly. You know enough. It was the merest chance that brought me in here.'

'Is there more to know?' Gilhooley asked narrowly. 'Could it be dangerous if I knew more? Is that what you're saying?'

'I'm not altogether sure what I am saying,' Corman confessed. 'You know enough for the safety of you and yours.'

Gilhooley grimaced, giving his right shoulder a twitch. 'You never gave me a bad order yet—nor advice if it comes to that. Another beer before you leave?'

'Another time,' Corman promised. 'Let's leave it at that. It's good to know you're home, mister, and still better to have met you again.'

'God bless you, Captain!' the big man responded. 'We fought in some rare fights.'

'Yes, we did,' Corman affirmed, offering his hand. 'And we won most of them too.'

Their hands met in the firm grip of old comrades, and they pumped arms with the deepest sincerity. Then, as their fingers parted, Corman turned away from the bar and strode out of the room, again conscious of the singer and admiring her latest song.

In the street, Corman freed his horse from the hitching rail and remounted. Fetching the brute round on the beaten way, he rode out of town over the ground by which he had come in. He sat leather with his reins held high and his mind racing. The pleasure of his meeting with Sergeant-major Gilhooley was still warming his innards, and he had the feeling now that the contact had been providential and might yet prove a saving circumstance. Yet it also seemed to him that, generally speaking, everything was still fluid and capable of flowing in any direction. If only his wretched imagination would not strive so earnestly to place things exactly. But that was how he was made, and he would have to put up with it. Better get back to his posse as swiftly as he could.

There was still plenty of the night to run, and he needed all the sleep he could get.

He cleared the town, and was getting ready to extract whatever gallop was left in his horse, when he perceived movement where a three-quarter moon was breaking cloud low to his right and casting its first cold rays towards the trail. Yes, there was a rider coming off the grass to the east. Not that there should be anything startling in that, yet the figure generated an inexplicable excitement in Corman's midriff. Checking his horse, he rose in his stirrups and peered hard at the advancing shape. Rufus Lebeau? Could it be? There was no reason why it should not, and perhaps he had been giving too little thought to that particular snake just lately. What in thunder could that man want here?

Hold still! The person coming in from the east was not the only one ahead of Corman, for the captain now made out another horseman before him. This second man was actually on the trail and halted in a posture which suggested that he was actually waiting for the first, and there was no longer any doubt of this when they raised their hats to each other and offered greetings in low voices, their heads bowing to a secretive angle as the first rider stopped beside the second and a conversation which was virtually inaudible to Corman began.

Suspecting that the second horseman could be Major Phileas Brock, Corman was calculating means by which he might get closer to the pair without being detected, when the talk ended and the speakers parted, the man that the captain believed to be Lebeau returning to the east and the other one wheeling away and going off northwards at a steady clip. Assuming the second man to be Major Brock, Corman imagined it almost sure that the Yankee—at this point for some liaison purpose which could only be guessed at for now—would be en route to rejoin his renegades at this moment. Doubtless the robbers were in hiding somewhere not too far off—and the possibility of a surprise attack on them later in the night was suddenly an obvious one—so the captain set off after the second rider, determined to follow him to wherever the renegades' camp might be.

FIVE

Corman rode stealthily and in a state of considerable unease. The three-quarter moon at his back was a blessing in that its silvery reflection off the clouds regularly touched the man ahead of him, keeping the other visible when the darkness of the north would readily have swallowed him normally, but it was also a curse, for Corman realized that, if he got too close and his quarry should happen to look round and make a careful study of the prairie in his wake, the pursuing horseman would be far more visible to him than the rider in front was to the captain. The risk was a big one, but Corman realized there was no choice other than to accept it. He must keep praying that no suspicion of pursuit would enter the mind of the man ahead, that haste would possess him utterly, and that he would be given no reason of any kind to look back until he reached his goal.

The white glimmer of the Pole Star was

a constant in Corman's furtive progress for about half an hour, and he was already beginning to wonder how much further away from his own people he would have to travel before he achieved the result he sought, when he perceived that his quarry was now swinging sharply to the left of North Point and climbing towards a low ridge which drew its dark line under the starry reaches of the west.

The gloom of the height immersed Corman increasingly as he neared the rim, and he was able to pick up speed and reduce the gap between himself and the rider before him with little to fear outside being detected aurally. But, careful to avoid the rumour of his presence carrying thus, he had got to within three hundred yards of his man when the fellow passed over the ridge and out of sight. He avoided the temptation of putting in what might conceivably have proved a disastrous spurt, holding back as previously, and he crossed the ridge about two minutes behind his quarry—meeting no challenge where he had feared that one might manifest—and now he found himself gazing down into the swimming dusk of a big hollow which the perceptibly shifted moon had just then lighted with the faintest silver and thus revealed the enclosing walls at a much lower level and water crossing the floor of the place.

The dark was spectral against the ground, and the air brooded. Corman felt a superstitious fear that he might step off the edge of the world as the underfoot angled steeply downwards. Checking his mount's progress with sharp jerks at his reins, the captain stayed in his saddle for a short while longer; then, his nerve failing him a trifle as the way down slanted even more acutely, he dismounted and began to feel a path on the largely unseen slope, toe kicking tentatively as he led his horse by the mouth.

The hundreds of feet of darkness under the nearer moonlight were nightmarish. They still sucked gently and beguiled. But then they lost something of their black magic as he picked out a tiny splash of fire amidst the crepe and realized that the renegades had made their camp down there. The spell lessened still further as he detected a stand of light timber on his right, and he decided to leave his horse in the cover of these trees and continue his descent unencumbered.

Halting his mount beneath what he

believed to be a sycamore, Corman secured the creature to a low bough and slithered on down the acclivity with increasing ease, for his eyes were accustoming to the blackness of the depths and his feet had convinced him that he need be afraid of nothing in his descent, since there were no pitfalls on the slope and its steepness was as much illusory as it was real.

The rose of flame, tiny from above, expanded into a considerable fire, and Corman saw the tents of a camp on the right of it and men wrapped in their blankets all about it. In the background a stream ran, just discernible to ear and eye alike, and there were trees and blotchy thickets present too, while a sentry leaned on his Springfield rifle at the front of the campsite and faced up the slope, nodding perceptibly and not far from sleep.

Corman was already getting near the guard. Fearing that he might be seen if any sound should suddenly startle the man wide awake, he side-stepped softly to the right and circled outwards, bringing himself into an oblique position from which he could peer into the camp with little chance of being spotted. Now that he was this near, he wondered why on earth he had taken so many risks to see the camp from this close up—for just discovering its location had really been enough initially—but there had been that curiosity in him as to the strength and quality of the people here, and there was, too, always that half recognised tendency in human nature to tempt fate.

Apart from the faint natural sounds of stirring leaves and tumbling waters, the silence down here was almost hypnotic, and Corman could easily have fallen into a kind of trance state as his eyes crossed tiredly. Amazed at his own reluctance to withdraw, he kept telling himself that it was long past time to get out of the hollow, but he was still there when somebody stirred in the nearest tent and a woman coughed restlessly. After that a man growled, and there were noises that suggested he had begun forcing himself on the female. This one made the captain sweat, and it did jolt him fully to himself. The devil take this filthy scum! He would like to string them up with his own hands. There were trees handy.

There was a sudden disturbance on Corman's right. It came from the nearside bank of the stream. Horses standing out of sight stamped and snorted their fright. Then a creature of some kind came running away from the water, shook itself, and dived uphill for the land at the top of the low. Seeing the nearby sentry stiffen and start turning towards the noise, Corman did the only sensible thing he could and dropped flat on his face in the grass. He lay motionless, all senses straining, and his heart banged and cold sweat broke on his forehead. Thus he lay there, just short of panic-stricken, knowing that the guard must come his way—praying, indeed, that the man had not already spotted him—and his right hand inched towards his gun as he prepared to roll on to his back and come up blasting.

Now footfalls dragged slowly in his direction, and the tension stank in his pores; but then the sentry's steps quickened and changed direction, the man doing a rapid shuffle up the slope beyond him and then halting abruptly. 'Pesky varmint!' he announced in the coarsest of voices. 'I'll warm your ass iff'n you—!'

'What the deuce was that racket all about, Biles?' broke in an educated male voice from the direction of the tents. 'Where are you man?'

'Over here, Major!' the previously enraged sentry replied meekly.

'Where? I can't see you. Get back to your post!'

'It was a coyote, sir!' the guard explained. 'I figure a cat must have chased it over the stream. That consarned critter sure spooked the horses!'

'And that's all?'

'Nothin' else, Major.'

'It isn't somebody on the prowl?'

'No, sir.'

'I hope you haven't been standing there half asleep, Biles?'

'Major!' Biles protested. 'Not a blade o' grass has turned but what I've knowed it. I've been wide awake as the day, sir!'

'I'll believe you this time,' the major said, clearly disposed to do anything but. 'Let us down, man, and I'll have you shot!'

'I hear you, sir!' Biles yelped.

Corman picked up the sound of a canvas flap falling back into place and knew that the major had retreated fully into his tent again. Then, his ears still preternaturally sensitive, he heard Biles complaining to himself that 'it was always him got it', and Major Brock was 'the worst bastard

87

unhung'. But, to the listener, the sentry's ire was the least of it, for Biles was obviously wide awake again and to stir a limb near him could prove suicidal just now. There was nothing for it but to continue lying low and to hope that the man would soon simmer down and become lethargic again, but that could prove a long job—and there was always the chance that a change in the guard would occur and further increase the camp's level of watchfulness—but it was all part of the inevitable state of things and the captain could only pray that it would eventually work itself out to his advantage.

The minutes went by and, as Corman had hoped, Biles, plainly a man of normally turgid body and mind, settled back into his lazy stance and soon became sleepy again; and, inside the next half an hour, the captain felt it had grown reasonably safe to start his retreat; so, staying almost flat, he eased himself backwards and round, taking himself uphill in the slowest of reverse creeping movements. For some time he lived with bated breath and checked reflexes—using up a seeming age to cover a few yards—but at last he knew himself well beyond the sentry's hearing range and carefully brought himself erect, using the shadows of the slope after that to speed his withdrawal and soon bring him to the place where he had left his horse tied. Then, having freed his mount, he led it up the last of the incline and back to the ridge above, crossing on to the prairie beyond with a gasp of relief and a nod of thanks to heaven.

Remounting, Corman now set off southeastwards across the grass, travelling downhill for a while and then passing into lonely miles where the sailing moon fully revealed the dark contours of the plain. It would have been easy to become slightly disorientated in the phantasmal state of the light, but the captain was blessed with a countryman's bump of direction and found little difficulty in locating the range fold where he had left his posse from Raftville to make camp.

Riding down into the tucked earth, Corman saw that his companions had built a fire with whatever fuel they could bring together and had made coffee. The remains of the beverage were still in their pot and hanging over the fire, and Frank Jessup—who was standing watch over the shadowy floor where the posse members were rolled in their blankets—said: 'It's still fit to drink.' Then he spat and slanted a questioning eye. 'You've been gone a long while, Brad.'

'More adventures,' Corman replied laconically, picking up a tin mug that somebody else had used, pouring himself a drink from the coffee pot, and pulling a face as he sipped. 'God—this stuff would be the death of a cottonmouth!'

'I prefer water.'

'Damn right!'

'What happened to you over yonder?'

Corman told him the whole of it, naming names where he could, and ending: 'We can make a quicker and cleaner finish to this business than we dreamed, Frank. If we fall on that renegade encampment around dawn—when everybody there is still three-parts asleep and thick of the skull—we can have the best of four times our number.'

'You think so, boy?' the Raftville baker queried. 'We're mostly ageing civilians, and they're trained military.'

'We can all hold our guns straight,' Corman answered, 'and a trained soldier dies as readily as any other man if he's shot in the right place.' Yawning, he considered his friend. 'Something else on your mind?'

'That guy you met in Bowie. The Irish sergeant-major—'

'Hank Gilhooley? Good man.'

'Well, can't you send into town right now and ask him to put together a posse of their best and join us out here?'

'You're losing sight of things,' Corman reminded. 'Like I told you, I'm pretty sure Rufus Lebeau is around. He's likely got a passel of no-goods in the offing. We can't tell what kind of watch he may have in Bowie by this time. It wouldn't be right to risk ourselves or the Bowie people at this stage. As far as we can be sure, we're completely free agents up to now. The responsibility is ours. We have guns enough, Frank, and we're not fools.'

'I ain't sure you should include yourself there,' Jessup said drily, 'but you do make sense right now.'

'I always make sense,' Corman sniffed, throwing out the dregs of his coffee. 'But if I don't get some sleep now, I'll be no good to anybody in the morning.'

'It must have been that knock on the head you got from Mike Magraw,' Jessup said unfeelingly. 'I wasn't that keen on sleeping when I was a young man like you.'

91

Corman turned a deaf ear. You couldn't argue with Frank Jessup when he was feeling contrary. The captain was done in, and that was that. In his life of late, you slept when you could, and this was the time for it; so he took down his blankets from behind his cantle and shot out the roll close to where the fire glowed and Mary Forbes was lying. Then he laid himself down and shut his eyes, sleep dissolving his consciousness as he seemed to hear again those sounds of brutal misconduct which had reached him from the renegade's tent an hour or two ago. The iron pierced still deeper into his soul. He'd pay those bastards tomorrow—and to blazes with the Yankees and their Jim Crow police!

But if Corman's sleep were deep and peaceful, his awakening was a rude one, for a volley of gunfire suddenly blasted down into his subconscious and shocked him instantly to his feet—others shouting out in fright as they sprang erect with him—and he sensed the presence of a full-blown panic which he could do nothing to calm. It was all happening too fast for that. The cry he sent up was an instinctive one: 'Mary!' And then he began blinking upwards with his sleep-sticky eyes at the gunflashes which were stabbing down at them from the upper edges of the range fold which contained him and his people.

'Brad?' the girl responded dazedly from his right elbow. 'Who—what is it?'

Corman's mind stuttered and ground, attempting to function clearly but failing to quite make it. It had to be—'Lebeau and company!' He felt disgusted with himself, for he had allowed fatigue to make him careless. It had never fully registered with him that, during the later stages of its closure on this spot, his posse's presence could have been spotted across the prairie by less than friendly eyes from Raftville. That was unforgivable, since the earlier attempt to bushwhack him should have provided a strong warning that Lebeau could be out with a force that was an actual threat to the hunters riding with Corman. Again, it had not been something that he could be sure of, but he ought to have been more imaginative, then erred on the side of caution. Now the annihilation of his party appeared to be in prospect. 'Your horse, Mary!' he ordered. 'Grab your horse!'

Fumbling almost blindly amidst the limbs and blankets flailing about him,

Corman located his own mount and started running it towards open ground beyond the fire. The guns were still cracking and booming, their flashes splitting the upper night like chain lightning on the rims of grass about the fold. Corman felt a slug whip the skirt of his coat, while another burned the saddle beside him, stinking. Nearby a man uttered a piercing scream, and his blood splashed warmly on the captain's face as his body fell. Shapes came and went, insubstantial as the waves of terror that swept the fold, and flame and sparks erupted as milling hooves kicked the campfire to pieces. Chaos and bedlam were hardly in it.

Corman peered through a billowing cloud of woodsmoke. He gained a glimpse of Mary Forbes trying to mount her plunging horse. He thumped the creature on the nose with all his force, steadying it at once; then, lifting at the girl's left elbow, set her astride its back. After that he swung up himself and, lashing at the rump of Mary's horse with his reins, got the brute moving ahead of him towards the exit from the land fold. Entering the narrows, they climbed where bullets laced, scrambling their horses to the upper ground and then flattening on the brutes' manes as they went hell-for-leather into the ice-splintered darkness of the frowning north, chased by more fusillades of lead from the shifting rifles behind them but missed by wider and wider margins.

It was not long before Corman realized that Mary and he were not alone. Two or three other members of the posse had managed to escape with them from the land fold. For all the volume of gunfire, the annihilation feared by the captain had not occurred. But the casualties were serious enough, and Corman's only thought was to ensure that nobody else should suffer death or injury for the present. To that end he led onwards, dedicating all to speed, and equine hair streamed in the following moonlight and divots flew. It seemed they would ride the Pole Star down. And they went faster yet when somebody yelled that a pursuit had started, while a random gun sent its confirming echoes rolling through the pallid south.

They galloped flat out for another mile or so, with everything at fever pitch, but the horses could only stand so much. Presently their efforts slackened and the chase became one of attrition, but that, too, lasted only a short while, for a bank of cloud snuffed out the moon and the prairie turned as dark as winter midnight. Cloaked now, Corman drew round to his left, the manoeuvre going on to describe a big semi-arc, for he planned to double back on the pursuers and by-pass them; but it was soon apparent that he and his companions had already lost their hunters in the natural course of things and that they were as much alone on the prairie face as they were ever going to be.

Corman drew rein, and his friends did likewise. The horses blew and surged nervously, steam fuming off their flanks. Rest and relaxation were the need of the moment, and all rested and relaxed. Then the captain asked: 'Who are we?'

'I'm here,' Frank Jessup said.

'Nicely,' Corman said. 'I know Mary's okay.'

'Yes,' the girl agreed. 'I saw Joe Sawyer fall.'

'They got Lute Kiln too,' another speaker said.

'Bill Tidy?' Corman queried.

'I'm here too,' Tony Sales announced, 'but Len Emery and Jem Tone are not.

They were nailed to the ground by them first slugs.'

'Four men,' the captain commented. 'It was cold-blooded murder.'

'Never should have been,' Tidy observed critically. 'Who the hell was on watch?'

'Kiln,' Jessup said. 'It's no good fixin' blame, Bill. Those killers would have snuk up on the long galoot. We weren't expecting anything, now were we?'

'Howsomever,' Sales groaned. 'I vote we go home, g'dammit!'

'What kind of talk's that, Tony?' Corman demanded. 'Give up doesn't come into it. We're still five. There's plenty we can manage.'

'Such as?'

'Leave that to me,' the captain advised.

'We're up against plenty,' Jessup observed. 'Tony and Bill don't know all.'

'You can tell them when we get riding again,' Corman said. 'It's not all bad. At least we know exactly what we're up against now. Rufus Lebeau is an active enemy—in up to his neck with those renegades—and good only for hanging. That goes for everybody with him. Remember, we still know where those robbers are—or I do—and we still have the chance to do

97

something about them.'

Sales growled negatively.

'Brad Corman's wife is in their hands!' Mary Forbes reminded sharply. 'As are Vesta Milligan and Jean Coltrane. We mustn't forget about them, Tony. They're good girls, and they deserve better than that!'

'Now that was well-spoken,' Corman approved.

'Brad?' Frank Jessup drew out thoughtfully.

'Yeah?'

'I still keep thinkin' about that sergeant-major you mentioned. Say what you will against it, we sure could do with some help from Bowie now. We don't have enough guns here to take on several times our number of desperate men.'

Corman opened his mouth to speak, then hesitated. He perceived the need to be very careful of what he said. He was conscious of Mary Forbes's presence as never before. Looked at with a clear eye, the odds were as hopelessly against them now as Tony Sales had suggested. Mary had come near tonight, and he did not want to end up getting her killed. He could see the way to getting her out of what lay ahead for the men, but she must not be allowed to think that he was trying to favour or protect her. He could already imagine the row that would occur if she believed that he was giving her preferential treatment because she was a woman. Yes, he'd got to attempt it—for the sake of his own conscience. But—where to start?

Then, unknowingly, Frank Jessup helped him out with a question. 'Do you figure Rufus Lebeau will keep chasin' after us in the wrong direction all night?'

'The rest of the night,' Corman corrected. 'Yes, I do. Maybe you were right just now. We could find ourselves with more prisoners from Major Brock's camp than the five of us could possibly handle. Perhaps we do need help from Sergeant-major Gilhooley—always assuming he can do a quick job of rounding up a posse around dawn. The folk in Bowie have neither seen nor heard anything to get alarmed about yet.' He made a clicking noise with his tongue, and sighed out his exasperation. 'Another point against is this. Hank Gilhooley is a drinking man, and people are never too willing to hear out a drinking man with what could be a tall tale. He could need help—the help of a young woman across whose lips strong drink has obviously never passed. What do you say, Mary? You'd be doing us all a big favour.'

'Who is this Sergeant-major Gilhooley?' Mary asked, plainly nonplussed. 'What are you talking about?'

Corman told her as much as he felt it was necessary for her to know, concluding: 'All you'll need do is find the man and tell him what I need. Then bring him and the posse back to the place I'll shortly start you from? Got it?'

'I'm with you,' the girl said, quite clearly not happy about it still. 'I'll do anything you want to the best of my ability. But are you sure you're not just trying to keep me out of harm's way?'

'Heaven only knows where harm's way is in this affair,' Corman said tightly. 'I could be sending you into worse danger than we're going into. I don't know. Work it out for yourself Or just believe in me.'

'You make it sound all right, Brad Corman,' the girl returned half accusingly. 'My business is revenge. You know that. I'm ready to spill blood for blood that's been spilled.'

'Will you shut up, Mary?' Frank Jessup

asked coldly. 'Somebody has got to go. You're the right person. Listen to Brad, will you?'

'I have done,' Mary Forbes said a trifle dismally. 'Oh, very well.'

'That's settled then,' the captain said crisply. 'We'd better not let these horses get chilled. Let's get going again.' He pricked his mount into a trot. 'Answer any questions back there, Frank.'

'If I can,' Jessup responded.

Corman shrugged to himself, aiming across the prairie now for the low ridge above the big hollow in which the renegades had their camp. You couldn't keep going into matters minutely—there wasn't time—but he had to admit that all this was not knitting up as clearly as he'd like. Yet events usually spoke for themselves, and what had to be done in association with them was in the main also obvious. All present would recognise the parts they had to play when the time came. He had few worries about that.

Before long they were riding against the tumbled skies of moonset, and the ridge which Corman was seeking appeared under the roiling tiers of pre-dawn cloud as a crayon-smudged line which could have been a lower part of the heavens. It was an illusory presence, seeming closer than in fact it was, and well over an hour went by—and the new day had started coming up—when the captain and his friends arrived under the crest. Halting, with the rim itself still one hundred yards ahead, Corman screwed round in his saddle as Mary Forbes rode up to him and said: 'This is where you leave us—and are to guide Hank Gilhooley back to. The renegades are encamped in the deep hollow on the other side of this rise. Do you think you'll be able to find this spot again?'

'Yes.'

'Bowie is pretty well due south of you.'

'I'll find it.'

'Scat, Mary!'

The girl departed, and the men watched her shape growing more and more indistinct as she moved into the south.

'She'll be all right, Brad,' Jessup said. 'We can rely on her completely.'

'I don't doubt it,' Corman answered. 'Now let's ride over the hump and do what we have to do.'

'Hell if I wouldn't rather bake bread,' Jessup remarked, as they began riding forward and upwards again.

Corman grinned at the soft laughter which greeted the sally. Leaning backwards in his saddle, he stretched his legs hard and caused his saddlestrings to sing. He, too, would rather bake bread—even if he didn't know how. Then they were over the land crest and heading downwards, the new light in the east reflecting off the midheaven and finding them on the upper steeps of their descent. The captain found the pitching presence of the earth hardly less frightening than on his previous visit to this place, and he dismounted without comment, noticing that his companions were not slow to do the same. Just being here required nerve enough—so why add to the test?

Picking a careful path, Corman deliberately led off to the right, arriving under the trees where he had secured his horse much earlier on. 'We can tie up here,' he said in a low voice as his companions grouped around him. 'If you look hard you can make out the campfire burning below us. It isn't all that far down. Check your guns.'

With the horses tied, the surviving possemen did as the captain advised, but they had hardly started descending again, when figures loomed out of the land about them and Rufus Lebeau's mocking voice said: 'Drop the hardware, boys! This is where it ends for you!'

Corman heard his shocked companions obey and, cursing through his teeth as the muzzle of a rifle jarred against his breastbone, he did the same, his Navy Colt falling between his feet.

SIX

The captain stood loosely as Rufus Lebeau's bulky shape approached him through the dawnlight. He felt a strong impulse to hit out, but knew that a bullet would carry his life away no sooner than his fist had made contact with the saloonkeeper's jaw. It was galling in the last degree, but he must accept what had happened here. He had been completely outthought, and Lebeau had the right to be cock-ahoop. All he could do now was exercise total self-control and stay alive as long as he could. When the tables had been turned, only a living man might get the chance to turn them back again.

'Wise man,' Lebeau approved, picking up the captain's revolver and thrusting it inside his own coat. 'I know what you wanted to do just then. That's right, Corman, behave—and you may live a little longer. A very little longer, of course.'

A second man walked up to Corman, and behind this one the captain saw the mighty shape of 'Iron Mike' Magraw looming. 'I owe you, polecat!' the second man declared, enough of his braids and rodent looks visible to identify him as Johnny Hiker, the Fort Worth gunman. 'Must say, though, you're a fair hand with a pistol for a nobody. You sure nipped a bit off my shoulder!'

'I thought it was you near the ford, Hiker,' Corman gritted. 'Next time I'll do the whole job.'

'Next time, says he!' Hiker jeered. 'You haven't a prayer, soldier. Why, I've the mind to gut-shoot you right here!'

'Don't upset the place,' Lebeau urged mildly. 'There are men sleeping below. Those Yankees need their beauty sleep.'

'Years of it wouldn't help the ugly sons-of-bitches much!' Hiker observed scathingly. 'If it weren't they're worth money to us, I'd pitch a stick of dynamite into that hog pen by the stream!'

'And kill those girls as well?' Corman spat.

'They're tainted whores by now,' Lebeau said dismissively. 'You wouldn't want your woman back again, would you, Captain?'

'Heaven's curse on you, Lebeau!'

'But I seem to have the blessing of hell, don't I?' Lebeau countered. 'Where did you go wrong tonight, Corman?'

'I was sure you'd have to tell me, mister,' the captain sighed disdainfully. 'It figures you saw us when we didn't see you. Around sunset, I'd say.'

'I have my field-glasses with me,' Lebeau said, nodding. 'I saw you leave your friends around dark and head for Bowie. It figured you wanted to find out if an attack had occurred on the town during the day. I'd have followed you into Bowie—with a view to doing you a mischief—but I had a prior meeting arranged with Major Brock. Then, later on, after we'd shot up your camp and I knew you'd escaped the bullets, it came to me that chasing after you at night was a waste of time and effort. After that, I got the idea—being somewhat fey—that you could have seen me talking to Brock just outside Bowie and followed him back to his camp.'

'That's how the boss told it to us too,' Johnny Hiker took over. 'He reckoned, if it was so—you being so all-fired chivalrous and the like—you'd judge you'd gotta do something about them girls in a hurry. Before events and we closed in on you this new day.' He chuckled villainously. 'You admit to the squeeze, soldier? Mr Lebeau sure had it all right, and it's worked out to our advantage like nothing else.'

'I have to admit it,' Corman allowed. 'I should have paid you more respect, Lebeau. But there's no touch of genius about it, and I should have seen the risks. I knew enough.'

'You did, Captain,' Lebeau agreed. 'You stand too high in your own opinion. Your father was just the same. He was *the* most obnoxious man.'

'Funny,' Corman remarked. 'My father said just the same thing about you. Only he was right.'

'Let me plug him, boss!' Johnny Hiker pleaded. 'That stinking mouth of his needs shutting once an' for all.'

'He's got nothing, John,' Lebeau said contemptuously. 'I expect you'll see him kicking before noon. Let's get these prisoners down to the camp. Put a jerk in it, Corman!'

Corman resumed walking down the slope. He felt Hiker's revolver start prodding at his spine. Glancing to his left, he discerned the figures of Bill Tidy, Tony Sales, and Frank Jessup keeping step with him. They had their heads down and were slouching along like beaten men. Corman couldn't blame them; everything seemed to have gone irretrievably wrong; but he could not subscribe to their sense of defeat. He straightened his own back and squared his shoulders, bringing his head up. No man was ever finally beaten until he admitted it to himself.

'Hey!' somebody bellowed out of the strip of darkness in which the stream ran across the hollow's floor. 'Is that you, Rufus Lebeau?'

'Fine soldier you are!' Lebeau shouted back. 'You are supposed to point your rifle and say: "Halt! Who goes there?".'

'That's enough of that!' announced a booming voice that Corman recognised as Major Brock's. 'What's happened, Lebeau? Do I perceive that you were right in that smart reasoning of yours?'

'Almost to the spot and the minute!' Lebeau declared smugly. 'We've captured our gallant Southern captain and what's left of his vigilance committee. They'll make a fine sight, decorating the trees!'

Corman entered the night lingering at the bottom of the hollow, but the darkness grew much less as his eyes adjusted to the scene about him. He soon discerned the major, clad in uniform coat and trousers, standing outside the nearest tent. Brock was big, round-faced, heavy of nose and moustachioed, in so far as Corman could see him clearly—almost the archetypal figure for his rank in the Union Army. The rankers whom Corman had last seen as sleepers were now sitting up in their blankets and undoubtedly trying, amidst their yawns and rubbing of eyes, to work out what exactly had been going on in their affairs during the hours of the past night. Over to the left, dim and threatening, stood a sentry with his Springfield rifle levelled, and the clicking of his teeth was audible as he chewed nervously at his wad of tobacco. 'Captain Corman, I presume?' Major Brock at last inquired, stepping forward to get a closer look at the Southern officer through the thin mist wreathing off the stream at the back of the campsite.

'That's my name, Major,' Corman acknowledged. 'Late of the First Texas Cavalry.'

'Brought in by a civilian,' Brock said scornfully. 'I might almost say taken in. You're a poor officer, sir!'

'But I haven't shamed my outfit, Mr Brock.'

'You're an insolent devil!' Brock fired back. 'What do you suppose me then?'

'A common thief.'

'Oh, yes!' the major ground out. 'I have a roving commission, Captain. The South has to be punished. To the victor the spoils, eh? Washington understands that.'

'Our people are aware you're just a renegade officer running a band of raiders,' Corman retorted—trying hard to retain the high moral ground, for he wondered if, despite the deeds of shame, Brock might even now get away with it at a Yankee courts-martial and be seen as no worse than a tough Federal officer performing a punitive duty in the north of Texas. The events of this time were still sufficiently confused to let him build a case on that.

'My doings are perfectly legal, Captain,' Brock insisted—'and I think you realize it now. While you, sir, have overstepped the mark. I understand, through Rufus Lebeau, that you have seen fit to take the law into your own hands. The practice of rough justice is permitted nowhere. It is indeed punishable by death under the jurisdiction of the Union, which I represent.'

'It all sounds fair and square to me, Major,' Lebeau said. 'Let's have an execution. The sooner these men are dead, the better for the South.'

'No, Lebeau,' Brock responded, his negative definite enough to brook all argument. 'I intend to make an example of these transgressors. We can do without a breed of Southern avengers springing up. It must be nipped in the bud. I'll execute them outside the courthouse in Bowie, and leave them hanging there for all to see. There's nothing like the bodies of hanged men twisting in the breeze to discourage rashness in others of their kind. I dare swear we'll have no more posses chasing us when the state of Corman's neck has been seen.'

'It's your decision, Major,' Lebeau said, his tones full of a fawning submission that yet failed to completely approve.

'You would rather see it done here?' the major asked narrowly.

Lebeau's shoulders heaved. 'I'm a practical man. The sooner they're dead, the sooner their threat ends.'

'Damn that!' Brock spluttered angrily. 'I have to infer that you think we can't be trusted to hold them. Guarded by my men, those prisoners would have a far better chance of escaping from the New York State Penitentiary.'

'Very well,' Lebeau soothed. 'But I don't reckon you'd disagree that they ought to be tied up?'

'Bind them by all means,' Brock said. 'I'll leave that to you and yours, mister.' He passed a masterful eye around the camp, daring any man present to blink, then kicked the soldier closest to his tent, who was still rolled in blankets, and barked: 'On your feet, soldier! Get the breakfast started. I want my coffee this minute!'

The entire camp came to life in an instant, and Corman was left in no doubt that Major Phileas Brock had total command here. Men scuttled this way and that, getting their beds rolled and tied, then more firewood was brought in and items of

112

food too. The fire was cheered up with a splash or two of coal oil, and large steel skillets were loaded with bacon and beans for the men and a few eggs for the officers. Coffee was crushed and set to steep, after which some of the soldiers shaved and all completed dressing. During the time all this went on, Corman and his friends were bound hand and foot by Lebeau and company, then left under a white oak to watch the spectacle of a camp breakfast in which they had no share. For, as Rufus Lebeau remarked sneeringly, men soon to die had no need for food. It was a waste to feed them.

With breakfast over, Major Brock, who had eaten in his tent, ducked into the open in full uniform, his hat square, and a cigar in his mouth. Eyes missing little that went on around him, he inspected his revolver, unloading and reloading it in the process. Then, holstering the weapon—one of the latest Colts, firing factory-encased bullets—he sidled through his seated soldiery to where Lebeau was sitting on a wooden box and finishing a mug of coffee. 'Rufus,' he said briskly, 'I want you in Bowie by the middle of the morning. That's the time most folk are out and about. You know what you have to do. Spread all the panic you can! Scare people silly! Tell any bloodthirsty yarn you like about what we do to folk! Make them believe we're just around the corner with sabres bare! Send every mother's son and daughter of them running for cover. It's worked fine around the countryside so far. We've yet to lose a man. It's the easiest of tasks to sack a virtually empty town and get out again fast!'

'Yes, Major,' Lebeau commented drily. 'I thought it all out pretty well, didn't I?'

'You haven't lost by it,' Brock reminded huffily. 'I don't want to hear about who thought of what. We could still function without you, but you couldn't without us.'

'Who did what soon becomes who's worth what,' Lebeau commented. 'That's what I want to avoid. That's what busts everything up.'

'Don't mention it then.'

'Then don't put us in second place, Major,' Lebeau advised. 'We know what to do.'

Brock bridled. He appeared on the verge of an angry outburst that might have resulted in a real quarrel between him

114

and the saloonkeeper; but just then a man clad in the uniform of a lieutenant in the Confederate cavalry stooped out of a tent on the major's right and stood flaunting his handsome presence; for he was a long-bodied, square-shouldered fellow, with a rakish, devil-may-care jib, and golden moustachioes that drooped to meet his jawlines. 'Morning, gentlemen,' he yawned. 'I heard what was going on—just now and earlier.' His eye picked out Corman and mocked. 'It's been a long time, Captain. I gather our new acquaintance is to be short. But that's to your disadvantage rather than mine.' Now he put a hand to his back. 'By heaven, sir—that wife of yours takes the seed out of a man like a pump lifting water! She gave me a night of it—she truly did!'

There was much haw-hawing around the campsite, and even the previously riling Brock looked amused, while Rufus Lebeau clapped his hands and called: 'Get her out here, Lieutenant Mapes! The captain should see his lovely wife once more before he leaves this world!'

'Anne, get your lovely hide out here!' the lieutenant ordered, reaching back into the tent behind him and pulling a proud-looking, dark-eyed girl into the open by her left arm. Clad only in frilly drawers and bodice, she let out a cry and tried to cover herself, but her eyes went at once to the bound Corman and shame flushed into her cheeks.

Subduing an eruption of awful emotions, Corman looked as understanding as he could and said quietly: 'It's all right, honey.'

Lieutenant Mapes turned his eyes to heaven and gave vent to a roar of incredulous laughter. 'By cracky! The man thinks she gives perforce!'

'That's right, Corman,' Lebeau taunted. 'Your good and faithful wife is a girl of appetites, and Jack Mapes has been regularly satisfying them.'

'Ever since you had me taken out of the shooting war, Brad,' Mapes agreed, 'and I was sent back to these parts in disgrace to commandeer horses for our cavalry. Anne and I have been real good friends, sir. But then we always did like the look of each other—even before she went to the altar with you. Didn't you notice on your wedding night? Tut, tut, my man!'

Maddened, Corman gave a great surge within his bonds, but the ropes would have held a gorilla as readily as he and his effort subsided almost at once and left a terrible weakness behind it. He, who wished to kill, was at everybody's mercy, and the camp's laughter swelled at him like a choking presence. 'I'll kill you for that, Jack!' he finally promised in a croaking whisper.

'If wishes were horses, Captain?' Mapes queried, an eyebrow raised as he twirled at his moustache with one hand while releasing Mrs Corman with the other. 'Get your dress on, Anne! Those Union dogs are straining at the leash! Don't you see them slavering?'

'You shame me, Jack!' Anne Corman protested brokenly, as she ducked back into the tent from which she had been dragged and threw down its concealing flap.

'Ah, women!' Mapes sighed.

'How dare you?' Corman breathed. 'How—how dare you treat her so?'

'Ware apoplexy, Captain,' Mapes warned. 'That face of yours! I've seen it before. A stroke is so nasty.' He tucked a thumb into his gunbelt, the lewd humour passing from his face and harsh lines of cruelty replacing it. 'She'll get over it, Brad—and she's mine. Let that be your dying thought!'

'You don't love the poor girl, Mapes,'

Corman observed, his drained body regaining a little of its strength and his voice becoming normal. 'It's just revenge. You've destroyed her to get back at me.'

'All is love to a woman,' the lieutenant remarked dismissively. 'I repeat, she's mine—and there's an end to it!'

'If I had named all the atrocities you committed up in Maryland,' Corman said bitterly, 'the high command would have hanged you.'

'Suppression?' Mapes wondered. 'Doesn't that make you as guilty as you would have everybody believe I am?'

'Be silent, the pair of you!' Major Brock interrupted. 'I'm of the mind to hang you both! The army of the South had its rascals all right. As witness, I suppose, the grey coats sitting here with the blue. But this is a sideshow. We have more important matters in hand than hurt feelings and female virtue. There are pockets to be lined. Ours!'

'Nothing more important than that,' Lebeau conceded. 'But I've enjoyed the sideshow. Didn't we have one of our own, Major? Where were we?'

'No more, Lebeau,' Major Brock cautioned. 'We can do without further flare ups. Take your men and leave my camp. I didn't want you settling in to begin with, but we don't always get what we want.'

'Force of events,' the saloonkeeper reminded shortly. 'Damn you then! But we do need each other, and it would be foolish to break up a good thing.' He rose to his feet, stretching in the tight, paunchy fashion of a middle-aged man who was too fat by half. 'Very well. Mike, Johnny—you others! Let's go. We're not welcome here.'

'You do your job, Rufus,' Brock said coolly, 'and you can depend on us to do ours.' He lifted a steadying finger, checking Lebeau and company that instant longer. 'Mid-morning, eh? We'll strike towards midday.'

Lebeau walked away, nodding; then, from a dozen yards up the slope beyond the camp—where a number of horses, obviously those belonging to the saloon-keeper and his men, were grazing loose—he looked back over his shoulder and shouted: 'We'll have the ropes hung ready for Corman and his friends!'

Major Brock said nothing more. Turning his backside on the receding figures, he went on smoking his cigar—a man who unquestionably had a lot on his mind nevertheless.

Corman, seeing all, felt his bitterly resentful interest in Lieutenant Mapes reducing as the man walked off into the waterside trees to the north of the camp—no doubt on some personal errand—and he now kept his eyes on Lebeau and company, watching the men catch their horses and mount up, then ride uphill towards the eastern ridge and over it in due course, leaving the scene in that direction bare for the moment and with nothing to hold his attention.

Easing his muscles against the knots that held them, the captain caught Frank Jessup's eye—for the man was hog-tied adjacent and showed signs of being near the end of his tether—and tried to pass a word of comfort; but a watching bluecoat sergeant put an end to that by kicking him in the ribs and pressing the muzzle of a rifle against his forehead. Wincing, Corman found himself thinking of his wife almost at once and remembering her humiliation. He didn't really wish to dwell upon any aspect of her presence just then, but soon discovered that he had a deep need to come to terms with her marital treachery.

He had never really understood Anne, and their domestic contact had been too brief for him to get used to her. She had still been something of a stranger to him when he had left their house for the war. She was a vivid person, he had perceived that, and capable of fiery expression in just about every direction, yet her responses to him had always been muted. There had been little passion in their relationship, and he had felt that Anne had submitted to him more as a matter of duty than because she wanted to. Yes, he had suspected that she had somebody else on her mind during their intimacies and, a rather inexperienced man himself, he had still been sensitive enough to recognise that she was no innocent. But he had never heard of anybody else to whom she had given her heart, and he had had more sense than to ask questions about her past.

He supposed the woman had treated him well enough in a distant sort of way, and he had been content to behave towards her more like a friend than a husband. He had assured himself that it would work out: that they would grow closer. But he was wiser now. Mapes? Would that limb of Satan have eventually crept out of the woodwork anyhow? Most probably. His pride recoiled from the thought, and he wanted to blame the war—as he had for so much else—but it was no good doing that. This was not a product of cause and effect any more than it was impersonal. It all had to do with secrecy and dishonest relationships.

Anne had refused to level with him. That was the crux of the matter. Perhaps she had just wanted marriage for itself as a social advantage—or to punish that tardy lover elsewhere. Yes, there had to be more to it than that. She had been alone too long, and she was a healthy woman with normal appetites. Many folk would have it that his failure to get home in four years was reason enough for anything that had occurred. They would say that he should have tried much harder to get the furloughs due to him. But something had always stood in the way of his getting back to Raftville. Time after time he had found himself a mighty important man to this general or that, and he had served well, yet he had always been ignored when the rewards were being handed out. Maybe that, too, had been in some degree his own fault. No leave, and no promotions. He had been a captain at the Junction, and a captain at the surrender. But that didn't matter. What mattered was this. Anne standing there guilty and humiliated—and Jack Mapes braying like an ass! He was smarting again, and felt like killing them both. Jack Mapes was no good, and Anne wasn't much better. Yet—he could pity the woman. A man's outraged sexual pride was a poor excuse for murder.

Then Corman laughed grimly at himself His plan was in train, yes; but nothing was sure—nothing was achieved yet. If Mary Forbes and Hank Gilhooley failed to arrive with help, he wasn't going to kill anybody. He was too tightly bound just now to raise more than his tongue in anger. Everything might still turn out in his favour, but so much could go wrong now. This way or that, he could be within sight of success and still get killed. His spirits went to a low ebb, and everything turned grey.

There was nothing for it but to suffer in silence. The taunting, unseen presence of passing time gnawed at him. His doubts and uncertainties were a plague at the middle of his head as he watched the soldiers present going off to attend to their horses and the cleaning tasks which winding up a camp entailed. They were already immersed in their day's work and, whatever the hours ahead might hold for them, they were at peace with themselves for the moment.

In the main the prisoners were ignored. They were left lying uncomfortably under the crumbling white oak where they had been dumped in the first place. The sergeant who had earlier kicked Corman had been confirmed as their guard. He continued watching them in a rather perfunctory manner, his rifle cradled across his chest as he sat on the box which Rufus Lebeau had earlier vacated. The non-commissioned bluecoat was a brutal-looking man, beetle-browed and stubbly chinned, with deep-cut lines around his eyes and dirty hair straggling down his neck. He wore a stained tunic and torn trousers, and everything about him suggested that war had reduced any finer nature he might once have had to nothing. To Corman's abruptly renewed horror, this man corroborated the impression he gave when a woman—known to the captain as

Vesta Milligan of Raftville—burst from one of the tents still standing nearby and shrieked that she couldn't bear any more, for the sergeant rose and took the legs from under her with a scything kick, after which he put a booted foot on her neck and pressed down hard as an almost naked man emerged from the relevant tent and stood looking down at the petticoated female, drooling tobacco juice and grinning inanely. 'Ain't she the purty one?' he giggled at the sergeant. 'You can let her up, Josh. I ain't done with her yet by half!'

The foot was lifted from the coppery Vesta's nape, and the undressed man grabbed at her as she started getting up; but she sent her head first one way and then the other, dodging beneath his grasp, then raised her hems and began running frantically out of the camp towards the slope that led up to the ridge. She was clearly bent on escape, but it would not have been too much for the sergeant to spring forward and put a stop to her attempt manually. Instead, as she reeled across the muzzle of his rifle, he pulled the trigger and the heavy bullet from the weapon appeared to tear through the woman from side to side, dropping her instantly. She lay utterly still and bleeding audibly, and there seemed no doubt that she was dead. 'You Yankee son-of-a-bitch!' Corman yelled at the man, raising up and kicking out with his bound legs in an effort to hurt the other. 'You cold-blooded, murdering Yankee son-of-a-bitch!'

'Hold your row!' the sergeant snarled at Corman, raking him across the mouth with the reeking muzzle of the newly fired Springfield, and the moment dissolved into ringing silence and glaring eyes.

SEVEN

Spitting blood, Corman fought to assimilate the pain of the blow that he had just received. His senses were rocking a trifle but he was still perfectly aware when Major Brock came running up from the camp with his revolver half drawn. The big officer demanded to know why the shot had been fired; then, seeing the prone female, he ran over and dropped to his knees beside her. 'She's dead!'

he announced. 'Why did you shoot her, Sergeant?'

'She was escaping, sir,' the sergeant replied. 'I was only obeying orders, Major. You said to shoot any prisoner who tried to run away. Standing order, sir.'

'Yes,' Brock admitted heavily, jacking himself erect with an expression of regret on his face. 'But all orders are carried out subject to common sense, man.'

'It was plain murder, Major!' Corman mouthed, salt fluid still trickling plentifully through his teeth. 'What kind of army does the Union run?'

'One much like your own was,' the major returned shortly. 'I do regret this. She was a nice girl, and I'll vouch for it. But done is done, Captain, and I can't punish a man for obeying orders.'

'I'd—'

'Yes, I know what you would do,' Brock cut in immediately. 'See it as it has to be—from my point of view. I must honour my own commands. No more, sir! If I were you, I'd spend my last hours making my peace with God. Or did you fight a blameless war, Corman?'

'This is the peace!' the captain protested.

Brock flapped a dismissive hand, his face

stony. 'Sergeant White, and you Private Blades—' this to the virtually naked man who had presumably been about to rape Vesta Milligan just before she had fled from him into the open—'pick that woman up and put her into the tent. Cover her with a blanket. We haven't time to dig a grave and give her a proper burial, but I'm sure somebody will find her before long and provide a Christian funeral.'

The sergeant saluted, then laid his rifle aside. He and the bare-limbed Blades did as they had been ordered, while Major Brock looked on. The removal and shrouding of the body took only a minute or two, then, satisfied all had been done that could be done, the major went back to whatever he had been doing before the shot was fired, while Sergeant White picked up his rifle again and Private Blades, his clothing draped over his left arm, trudged off into the nearby greenery to rejoin his comrades.

Corman was still furious at what had happened. He wanted to fly at the murderous White again. But, aside from the certainty that a new verbal assault would only get him some more mistreatment, he realized that all had been said that mattered and that no words of his could possibly influence the brutal sergeant or bring Vesta Milligan back to life. The woman's killing had been just another dreadful incident to put with the rest. In fact Frank Jessup put the lid on the matter when he said: 'God rest her soul.'

'Amen,' Corman agreed; but the listening sergeant simply blew a raspberry.

They settled as best they could, and the captain was again uneasily conscious of time moving relentlessly onwards. He was also aware of being very thirsty. He had had little to drink during the last twenty-four hours, and the coffee that he had consumed last night in the land fold had been no thirst quencher. His tongue was beginning to stick to the sides of his mouth, and the sound of the running water nearby started to play on his nerves and his dehydrating tissues alike. Then, as this minor suffering threatened to turn into something worse, the sound of distant gunfire thrilled through his head and he wondered breathlessly what it could be about—if not a meeting between Rufus Lebeau's party and a force that Mary Forbes, with the help of Hank Gilhooley, had managed to raise in Bowie. This could be the beginning of the end for the renegades and, his thirst and all his earlier worries falling away, Corman shared a wink among his companions who were braced in their bonds and looking at him delightedly.

Corman glanced covertly at Sergeant White. The Federal n.c.o. had clearly heard the gunfire echoing in at the same time as the prisoners, for he was already moving hesitantly in the direction of the sounds and had a puzzled look on a face that became more and more vacuous the harder he listened. But he wasn't alone in his listening pose for long, for his comrades came running up from several points in and around the campsite and joined together in similar states of frowning concentration. Major Brock joined them almost at once, and Lieutenant Mapes also put in a quick reappearance, his mystification equalling that of the other renegades present. 'It's almost bound to be something to do with Rufus Lebeau,' the major observed, speaking in the kind of voice that was intended for everybody. 'It was early when he left us, and he would naturally have stopped somewhere out on the prairie to let a bit of time go by. It

130

isn't so far to Bowie, and he was not to enter the town until mid-morning. Can he have run into trouble?'

'We've got to assume it,' said Lieutenant Mapes. 'But what kind of trouble, Major? Can it concern us?'

'If it concerns him, Mapes,' Brock reflected, 'it almost certainly concerns us. Have we overlooked anything?'

'I don't see what,' Mapes frowned.

'I require a galloper,' Brock said.

'You've got one,' Mapes responded.

'All right,' the major barked. 'We'll not stand upon procedures. You have the best horse. Ride up on to the plain and find out what that shooting is. Then get back down here as quickly as you can.'

'Lickety-split, sir!' the lieutenant promised, turning away and loping into the greenery on the north of the campsite—his disappearance amidst the new leaf one of a minute only; for he reappeared beyond the streamside growth on a sleek chestnut mare that had obviously been saddled and awaiting his pleasure and went pounding uphill towards the eastern ridge. Despite the angle of the ascent, Mapes's horse seemed to cover the ground effortlessly and it was no time at all before the rider

131

touched the sky and then dropped over the ridge, his departure long since silent and now a matter of uncertain memory.

The distant shooting, intense for a short while, had become sporadic, and the galloper hadn't been out of sight for very long when it ceased altogether. Major Brock said nothing more concerning it, but he stood looking fixedly upwards and rasping nervously at his chin. The now elated Corman was pleased to witness the major's lack of activity, for Brock—unknowingly, of course—was playing into the hands of the attackers he could hardly anticipate. If he could but know with certainty what was happening, he would realize that the hollow was a natural trap and get out of it at top speed. The formation appeared to have no back door, and any men who took up firing positions on the height above would act like the stopper in a bottle to those contained by the walls of the low place. Major Brock could end up in a virtually impossible position.

Five or ten minutes went by. The men stood around as before and the tension gathered. Nobody gave the captives a glance, for all eyes remained glued to the ridge. Then three riders came dipping over

132

the crest above, and Brock and company surged instinctively to meet them, leaving the campsite itself and straggling somewhat upon the grass beyond. Eyes straining upwards, Corman certainly made out the figure of Lieutenant Mapes again and believed the other two horsemen were Rufus Lebeau and Johnny Hiker respectively. If the evidence could be trusted, it appeared that Lebeau had lost 'Iron Mike' Magraw and the rest of his men and, from the extreme haste the three were exercising, it seemed a fair bet that pursuers were hot on their tails. Corman quivered all over with the strain of it as he waited for the men who could only be riders from Bowie to show on the height above.

But then there was movement in the apparently empty camp itself. The captain turned his head quickly towards it. He saw a woman's figure crawling rather slowly across the ground towards him and his trussed up friends. His gaze deceiving him for that second—or his mind playing a trick—he thought it was Anne, his wife, making for them, but all at once he noticed the bloody stain upon the back of the female's petticoat and realized with a strong sense of shock that he was looking at Vesta Milligan whom they had all supposed to be shot through and dead. The woman was chalk white and all eyes, but there was about her a hint of purpose which denied her apparently fatal injury, for she carried a hunting knife in her right hand and had the obvious intention of cutting the bound men from Raftville free.

His scalp tingling over his throbbing brain, Corman felt the sweat running down his face as the woman crawling across the grass drew closer and closer. She looked resolute, but far from a bundle of energy, and it would need only one man over there to turn his head and she and her purpose would be instantly at risk. Now that—aside from the damage it would do his immediate hopes—struck the captain as something awful to contemplate. For Vesta to have survived a seemingly mortal shot, only to be fired at for a second time just after she had revived, would be the kind of dark trick that Fate reserved for the very few.

It didn't happen. The woman safely reached the white oak and the men who were tied up beneath it. She said nothing;

but, raising her torso as best she could and breathing a trifle wheezily, thrust the blade she was carrying into Corman's bonds and turned it until its edge started to bite, sawing after that with grim determination until a round of the rope parted and Corman was able to start exerting his muscular strength to help her free him. Bracing, and then giving his arms a sudden wrench, the captain cleared his upper body of the trussing hemp and shook and kicked his legs thereafter until the last of the bonds flew away from him and he was able to scramble up stiffly and take the knife from the exhausted Vesta's hand, using it to cut his male companions free during the next ten or fifteen seconds. 'Done, by heaven!' he gasped, expressing his sheer relief.

But this new elation was short-lived. For Vesta Milligan gave a little cry and pointed feebly towards the land at the foot of the slope adjacent. Corman's jaw swivelled quickly, and what he saw caused his heart to sink, for Sergeant White must recently have peered round and glimpsed something that he so far deemed no more than suspicious amidst the morning shadows under the white oak. But now, frowning, the sergeant brought his rifle to the ready and began returning to the camp site at an accelerating run. 'Keep right down!' Corman breathed, judging that the Federal n.c.o. would need to get a good deal closer yet before he could be sure of what he beheld.

Eyes darting and head on the shift, White came on to within a few yards of the oak; then, his gaze widening as he perceived what had actually occurred, pulled his rifle into his shoulder and began to peer along the sights, aiming for the captain. Praying that the sergeant wouldn't cry out—or squeeze off prematurely—Corman did the single thing he could and rose to his knees, hurling the hunting knife at White with all his force. Happily, the emergency throw was a completely accurate one, and the sergeant took the point of the heavy blade in the middle of his chest and toppled over backwards, only a low gasp issuing from his mouth. Spreadeagled upon his spine, he gave one convulsive kick and then shuddered into a stillness that could only be death.

Crouched over, Corman closed on the body, his eyes watching the backs of the soldiery as they continued gazing towards the ridge. Now he tugged the knife out of the sergeant's heart, wiped the blade on the n.c.o.'s coat, and thrust the weapon into his own belt. After that, working at the level of speed that only fear could induce, the captain removed the dead man's military gunbelt and buckled it around his own waist, unbuttoning the flap of the holster and leaving an open path for a quick withdrawal of the pistol within should circumstances suddenly demand it. Finally, he picked up White's Springfield-Allin rifle and helped himself to the dead sergeant's cartridge pouch, this appropriation of weapons and ammunition bringing him a renewal of confidence in his own powers.

Creeping back to the copper-haired Vesta Milligan and his three male friends, he said: 'Don't let's hang about like nitwits! Let's get the hell out before Brock and his other men cotton to what's happened over here!'

'Where to, Brad?' Jessup asked defensively. 'It's all of a piece down here, boy.'

'We have a mite of cover,' Corman reminded him. 'We can lead them a dance maybe. They've got all sorts of trouble to come, you know. They may not be able to pay that much attention to us. Anyhow, let's get out of sight.' He glanced down at Vesta Milligan, who was crouching on all fours. 'Tidy—and you, Sales—help this girl!'

'Leave me where I am, boys,' the woman whispered. 'I'll only be a burden to you.'

'Nonsense!' Corman snorted. 'If we live, you live. Those bastards—begging your pardon!—will certainly kill you if we leave you here.'

With the two men named supporting the injured woman, they all moved to Corman's left—southwards—around the back of the white oak and on into the undergrowth beyond. It was not the captain's preferred direction, since he had thoughts of circling to reach the horses—which he and his three male companions had left high up on the northern side of the hollow during the night before—but to have gone to the right would have meant crossing the whole campsite in the first place and then intruding on the ground where the horses belonging to the renegades were picketed in the second. And between the possible results of the exposure and the noises that startling the mounts might have caused, it was unlikely that they would have managed to reach the northern side of the low and then sneak out of the greenery into the climb beyond without being spotted. Whatever they'd done, however, could hardly have benefited them much if the robbers should start hunting them in earnest. But Corman nevertheless felt that they still had a slightly better chance of surviving in the present circumstances by moving southwards in what cover there was along the bank of the stream.

Yet, while believing that they must push on, the captain still allowed himself to be diverted from his purpose when shouted conversation reached his ears from the foot of the slope nearby. Checking both himself and his companions, he peered back through a gap in the undergrowth to where Lieutenant Mapes and the two other riders who had come down from the prairie with him—Rufus Lebeau and Johnny Hiker indeed—were still sitting their horses and urging Major Brock and the soldiery behind him to run for their horses and leave the hollow immediately. 'A posse from Bowie has been set on us,' Mapes explained. 'There are some men in it that I recognise. Fellows from crack

Confederate regiments. They really know one end of a gun from the other!'

'I find this—this preposterous!' Major Brock spluttered. 'How the deuce could those people possibly have known we were down here, Lebeau?'

'I think it's something else we can blame Captain Corman for, Major,' Lebeau answered. 'Mary Forbes, a pert miss from Raftville, is among the leaders of that party up there. She clearly survived our guns when we attacked Corman's posse last night, and the captain must then have sent her into Bowie for help.' He drew breath and gestured. 'It's all gone wrong, Brock. We were never as safe as we thought!'

'Damn that for a yarn!' the major seethed.

'Hot damn to you, sir!' Johnny Hiker called cheekily. 'It's no good standing there with your big Yankee mouth gaping. To horse, you fool! The prairie is the only safe place today—because it's so goddam big!'

'Look!' one of the soldiers shouted. 'They're up there, Major—strung out along the ridge!'

Gunfire crackled on the height, and Corman heard a couple of spent bullets drop into the greenery a few yards away.

'We'll stand them off!' Major Brock declared. 'We are trained soldiers, and they're a civilian rabble. We must win, men!'

'Major—Major!' Lieutenant Mapes cried. 'Those men are not going to gallop down the hill and let you use them as targets! They'll contain you, sir, and starve you out if they have to. They've got the patience of Job when it's necessary. I'm telling you!'

'How dare you, Mapes!' Brock raved. 'We'll talk about this!'

'For ten years if you like!' the lieutenant fired back. 'Aren't you listening?'

Brock swung away, purple of cheek and clearly lost for words. 'Horses, men!' he roared, decisive at long last. 'We stop for nothing! We'll charge our way out of here!'

The listening Corman grinned triumphantly. It was turning out exactly as he had hoped. Indeed it could not have worked better for him and his friends. The prisoners seemed to have been completely forgotten by the renegade company in the near panic that was sweeping it, and Corman did not believe there would be any last moment attempt to visit either the oak tree or the tents. The danger was over for now, and their enemies would not think of Corman and the Raftville people again until they had extricated themselves from their present plight. If they did. And the doubt was real enough.

EIGHT

Keeping motionless, Corman held his position among the trees and bushes which surrounded him. He urged the people with him to do the same, fairly certain by now that there was no need to continue their flight. It should not be long before they had this part of the hollow more or less to themselves. Then they would be able to return to the campsite in safety and have no difficulty in fetching his wife out of the tent in which she had been imprisoned and also find no problem in locating the third woman kidnapped from Raftville. Nothing had been seen or heard of Jean Coltrane so far, but he did not doubt that she would appear soon enough when he called her name among the tents.

'There they go, Brad!' Frank Jessup

announced excitedly, his fingers gripping the captain's right elbow with force enough to hurt.

'Sure,' Corman said laconically, shaking off the other's grasp. Then he watched Major Brock leading out of the growth to the north of them and spurring into a thunderous, yelling gallop which bore him and his renegade band up the land towards the eastern ridge in a fearsome cluster. 'Wait until the guns up there start to shoot.'

It made a brave sight as the bluecoated riders surged towards the summit, some of them flashing sabres and others triggering sidearms—and it appeared that they must frighten the best and carry all before them—but then a blast of rifle-fire, unexpectedly disciplined and intense, rattled out along the ridge, showing as a line of vivid red streaks and abrupt puffs of dark gunsmoke, and the horsemen rushing uphill seemed to run into an unseen wall and riders and mounts tumbled, many of them upending and bringing down others as they toppled themselves. Yet, heavily checked—and with what had to be numerous casualties in their wake—the survivors of the fusillade heaved and threshed onwards, trying to force the height on courage and muscle alone, but the wave gradually broke, collapsing at its centre and falling away at its ends, and Corman recognised that the charge had been the failure he had thought it might and would not be repeated.

Now the questions were: Who among the bluecoats had survived?—and what would those survivors do next? It had become another of those fluid and abruptly changed situations, and Corman reacted to it far more by instinct than any important change in his earlier reasoning. 'Let's get back to the camp!' he urged.

'Hey?' Jessup queried, staring in surprise. 'We have business there?'

'My wife and Jean Coltrane,' Corman answered, knowing the names would be explanation enough in themselves.

'Got you,' Jessup said. 'Them hellions could use the girls as hostages now.'

'Human shields,' Corman agreed, for the baker's thought had already flashed across his own mind. He was about to add that it might depend upon who among the renegade leaders was left alive—if any one of them—as to whether that course was pursued or not, but he perceived before another word left his lips that the same tactic could be employed by the highest or the lowest of the renegade band alike, depending on who had the intelligence to discern it. So the captain simply beckoned, and he and his companions hurried a return to the campsite as best they could, Vesta Milligan notwithstanding.

They broke upon the ground where the tents stood with anxious faces and some noise. Corman was not too surprised to see his wife standing in the open, beside the ashes of the fire indeed, though his attention soon shifted to the battered canvas erection next to that which Mrs Corman had occupied, for the brown-haired Jean Coltrane was peering out of its door and looking faintly bemused. Then, her eyes widening at the state Mrs Milligan was in as she drooped between the supporting figures of Bill Tidy and Tony Sales, Anne Corman exclaimed: 'Vesta! I thought—I heard—Oh, what has happened to you, honey?'

'That brute of a Sergeant White shot me,' Vesta Milligan gasped. 'I reckon the bullet must have creased my spine. I went out like a light, Anne, and now my legs are full of pins-and-needles and not much help to me.'

'Brad?' Anne Corman asked.

'Take it as she tells it,' the captain returned, not sure whether he had understood the reason for his wife's question mark or not. 'You'll have to look at her wound when you can.'

'What's happened?'

'Plenty,' Corman responded. 'I figure you'll have heard what mattered. It's now that concerns us.'

'What do you mean?'

'Fancy serving as a hostage to those devils who kidnapped you, Anne?' the captain demanded stonily. 'I'll bet you don't! Camp women don't die of the experience, but it's different with human shields.'

'Brad!'

'Don't play the injured innocent with me,' he snapped. 'I know all about it, don't I?'

'All?' she asked bitterly.

'Enough then,' Corman said, his voice heavy and dismissive. 'You don't imagine that Jack Mapes loves you? He doesn't know the meaning of the word! If he's still alive, he'll use you any way he can.'

Anne Corman said nothing, but her face admitted that she feared she had just heard the bitter truth.

'Save it, Brad,' Frank Jessup cautioned, taking from the captain's hand the rifle that Corman had lifted from Sergeant White's body and been carrying ever since. 'I'd better have this.'

'I guess you had,' Corman conceded, glancing to his right and looking up the slope beyond to where he was able to make out the unmistakable figures of Major Brock and Lieutenant Mapes as they emerged from a mill on the upper part of the incline and went into full retreat, their horses racing downhill after one or two others that had also turned into flight. The guns higher up flashed and banged behind the pair but, while a rider ahead of them fell, the major and lieutenant came pounding on down until they were out of accurate shooting range.

'Want me to have a try at that pair o' skunks?' Jessup inquired, drawing his hammer on the big cartridge in his rifle's breech.

'You'd most likely miss,' Corman responded—'and so would I. There's no sense calling attention to ourselves just now. Those two probably can't see us from where they are.' He threw glances all around him. 'Let's get the women away.'

'Say where, dammit!'

'All right,' the captain said, a bit nettled. 'Let's do the unexpected. By the sound of it, that stream back there is no great depth. Let's cross over to the land on its other side. There's a fair piece of it between here and the cliffs yonder. If we can stay loose long enough, I reckon those people from Bowie will get an idea of what's happening and come on down and rescue us—if there's a need.'

'Makes sense,' Jessup acknowledged.

Turning about, they covered the few yards to the stream at the back of the campsite. Corman saw at once that his judgment concerning the depth of the flow was a correct one. The waters in the channel ran fast, but were less than eighteen inches deep, and the bottom itself—though covered in places by jutting rocks—was of a grey shingle that looked firm enough. Crossing over should be easy, and they need anticipate nothing worse than wet feet.

Picking Vesta Milligan up in his arms, Corman stepped down into the stream and

148

waded the four paces through the chill waters to the opposite shore. There he put Mrs Milligan down on the bank—which was about two feet above the level of the flow—and climbed out himself, while his unburdened companions joined him in the next minute. After that, crouched and watchful, they stood together listening again, and all stiffened as a still moderately distant but all too familiar voice—that of Lieutenant Mapes—shouted: 'We can't afford to be noble, Major! We must use Anne Corman and the Coltrane woman as hostages. Let's get them out of the tents. The people from Bowie won't fire on us if we're carrying girls in front of us on our saddles!'

'I can't see it either!' Brock approved. 'You fetch the women. I have another errand. I mean to shoot those prisoners we left down here.'

'I'm sure Corman deserves punishing for the trouble he appears to have caused us,' Mapes agreed.

The unseen riders must be getting close now. Corman saw a clump of mesquite over to his right and about a dozen yards back from the edge of the stream. He pointed to the shrubs. 'Let's get out of sight behind those bean trees,' he urged. 'With any luck, Mapes and Brock will think we're still on their side of the water when they find the women are missing and go to work accordingly.'

With Tidy and Sales again helping Vesta Milligan, the six of them hurried in the direction which the captain had indicated, and they moved in behind the shrubs and became invisible to anybody looking across from the nearby stream's eastern bank. Finding himself a small gap in the leaves before him, Corman peeped through and watched the ground beyond the water on which the tents stood. His nerves began to thrill with anticipation.

Then he saw Brock and Mapes come riding on to the campsite. The men drew rein, startlement showing at once in their postures. Then they swung down fast and went running over to where Sergeant White lay with the knife wound in his chest. 'He's dead, Mapes!' Major Brock declared, his voice loud and snarling. 'And Corman and the other prisoners appear to have been cut free!'

Lieutenant Mapes made an angry gesture, then went over to the tents and started looking into them one after the other, passing across their doorways and ripping at their entrance flaps with a faster and faster hand. 'Gone, by heaven!' he raved. 'What the deuce went on here, Brock?

'Even the dead woman's body has gone!' rasped the major, who was following Mapes in a similarly brisk and enraged pantomime. 'Corman and the others must have taken it with them!'

'Was she dead?' Mapes queried.

'Of course she was dead!' Brock retorted, a perceptible tremor of doubt in his voice for all the emphasis. 'Didn't I examine her myself?'

'Examine?' the lieutenant queried—'Or look at? I've seen men who were sodden in blood get up after the battle and walk off. Some are still alive today!'

'Well, Vesta Milligan is gone,' Brock said far more soberly, 'and that's that, Lieutenant.'

'One of the men who visited her tent for a little pleasure could have left some of his equipment behind—a knife among it,' Mapes reflected. 'If Mrs Milligan wasn't dead—'

'You speculate, sir!' Brock interrupted, testy again.

'What if I do, Major?' Mapes asked, snapping his fingers inconsequentially. 'We may never know the answer. But one thing is certain. The escapers are still down here, and they can't be far away. It's still within our power to locate those women and kill the men. We've got to do it, sir. It's the only certain way we have now of staying alive.'

'Do you suppose I don't realize that, Mapes?' Brock demanded as he glanced around him, arms akimbo and frustration revealing itself in every line of his body. 'Let's see.'

Corman drew his head back from his peep-hole in the mesquite foliage before him, and Frank Jessup, who had found a similiar tiny aperture for himself, made a small but ominous shift in the position of the rifle which he was holding. 'Listen to 'em squawk!' he hissed. 'They're alive this minute only by your grace, Captain. We can still nail 'em easy as you like. Why don't we up with our guns and do it, son?'

'Listen to you!' Corman gritted in retort, scowling. 'It's another case where you're right so far as it goes, but only that far. We don't know how many of Brock's soldiers lived through that charge on the ridge and may still be near the major now. What the officers can think of, the men can too. We don't want to stir up a hornets' nest unless we must. Think of the women! We must protect them as much as we can.'

'Sure, you may be right,' Jessup groaned, clearly doubting. 'Maybe you think a mite too deep about it.'

'Maybe that's your lack, Frank,' Corman temporised.

'Brad, the chances you scorn never come again.'

'It's not my habit to scorn any damned thing,' the captain returned, once more peering intently through the mesquite as he saw Major Brock swing a beckoning arm and heard him start shouting orders again.

'You men over there! Come to me!'

Corman watched five or six soldiers ride on to the campsite. Whether they were the only men who had survived the recent charge on the ridge, he could not be sure, but no others appeared. Major Brock lined them up before him, then, using a lowered voice which the listener could not entirely follow, explained what seemed to have happened here and swiftly added what he now wanted done about it; and the bluecoated men dismounted as he finished speaking and ducked away into the greenery to the south of where the tents had been erected, probably acting out the same line of reasoning which had influenced Corman while he and his friends were essaying escape in that direction.

Major Brock went off with his men, pursuing them with a doubled back and pistol in hand, but the peering captain saw Jack Mapes—perhaps on his own say-so—run off the campsite northwards, obviously intent on eliminating the inferior possibility that the escapers could be attempting to get away over the green but soaring wall by which the stream entered the hollow through the low and daunting presence of a tunnel. Mapes, too, vanished almost straightaway and, while Corman recognised the risk that he and his companions might be spotted at some juncture through the gaps in the waterside growth on either side of the camp, he decided that it was time to move out of their presently too vulnerable hidingplace almost on top of the stream and retreat into the morning gloom under the westerly turn of the confining bluffs behind them. Aside from anything else, there was a good chance that the shadow of the cliffs would absorb their presence to all but a glimpse by the direct eye, while he was still hoping that the natural fixity which so often afflicted the human mind would continue to restrict the enemy's thinking to the notion that he and his friends must still be on the eastern bank of the water because everything had happened there so far. 'Okay,' he said, jerking a thumb towards the retreating turn of the rockfaces. 'But careful now. Let's keep this clump of mesquite between us and Brock's men for as long as we can.'

Backing off cautiously, they cleared the cover of the bean trees and soon entered the damp, scree-strewn land that formed a sort of drab carpet along the foot of the western bluffs. Now they sidled to their left, Corman having no definite purpose just then—except to remain free and avoid being spotted—and they let the bend of the rearing cliffs away from the stream take them with it.

The extreme back of the depression appeared before them. This took the form of a tuck in the dark stone wall on their left which had not been visible previously from any of the positions which they had occupied in the hollow up to now, and it was with genuine surprise that they found themselves looking round a kneeling buttress and then gazing up a gritty, boulder-studded acclivity which had stairlike features about it and grassy overhangs on either side of its diverging egress at the top.

Corman studied the formation for any faults, though he felt sure already that he and his friends had come upon a comparatively easy way out of the hollow. There was nothing to worry about up there, and he thanked the gods of good chance for this latest boon. If they climbed out of the hollow here, they should be able to place themselves beyond any more danger from Brock and Mapes in quite a short time. 'Figure you can make it to the top, Vesta?' Corman asked of the injured woman as she gazed upwards with the rest.

'I'm sure of it,' she answered firmly. 'I'm feeling a lot better. My legs are getting strong again.'

'We believe she's suffering more from shock and loss of blood than anything,' Jean Coltrane said, speaking for Anne Corman and herself, both of whom as a natural circumstance had a much greater intimacy with the wounded female than had the men.

'She was lucky,' the captain acknowledged. 'So—would you people'—this to the two unhurt women and Bill Tidy and Tony Sales—'like to make the climb first? You can all give Vesta a hand as you think best. I'll be right behind you to offer support if things start to go wrong. Frank Jessup can bring up the rear with his rifle. Just in case we need cover.'

Jessup gave a sardonic sniff. 'Don't talk it up, Brad!' he chided. 'We should be out of everybody's sight round this corner.'

Corman nodded. It appeared that this character difference between him and the baker, where caution was necessary, was becoming more pronounced. He wanted to remark it to Jessup, but felt that the matter was unworthy of notice, so he stood back and watched as the majority of the party began their ascent, only starting to climb himself when he was sure that the others were established on the slope and that it was safe for him to take his first steps.

The climb wasn't quite as undemanding

as it had seemed at first sight, for it was much steeper than its stepped areas made it appear. There was a certain amount of scrambling to it, and knees had to be bent and steadying hands lowered to avoid slippage on the patches of rubble and dusty erosion at the middle stages of the ascent. In order to protect themselves fully, individuals often had to give all their attention to themselves, and this meant that Vesta Milligan was left once or twice to fend almost completely for herself, but she managed without mishap and Corman was forced to step up and provide nothing dramatic by way of help from the rear.

The captain's wife and Jean Coltrane were the first ones to reach the top. Jean kept low upon the rim, but Anne stood tall against the sky and looked back and down. Corman wondered for the moment if she had taken leave of her senses, since he feared that she might be on view to anybody gazing upwards from the ground where the hollow's stream flowed. He was tempted to shout at her—fearing some form of treachery on her part, though unable to believe in it for obvious reasons—but he realized the danger that his voice would carry to the soldiery back there and did no more than keep quiet and scowl upwards.

Then a shot cracked out from below, and a bullet skipped at Corman's right heel and sang, its flight ending in an audible thud against a sandstone riser not a dozen feet beyond him.

'Dad-blast it!' Jessup swore, and his rifle boomed.

Craning, Corman peered towards the bottom of the ascent. He saw Jack Mapes standing there, revolver pointing upwards and gunsmoke swirling around his head. The grey-coated lieutenant's pistol spoke a second time, and the slug cut deep into the dirt at the top of the slope and stuck. Fumbling out his own revolver, Corman twisted round and poised there, uncertain of balance, and triggered in reply, missing as he had feared he must, and Mapes's Colt blazed for the third time and Frank Jessup—who was fumbling a cartridge into the breech of his army rifle—gave a dull cry and pitched the heavy weapon away from him, clutching at his midriff and falling to meet the angle of the slope. He slid several feet downwards on his jaw and belly, coming slowly to rest, then lay inert and bleeding steadily into the light debris that slurred around him.

Scrambling downwards to where the baker lay, Corman fired and fired again at the ducking and dodging Mapes—who had presumably spotted the escapers from the northern part of the streamside greenery some minutes ago and started in their direction at about the time they had begun climbing—and the lieutenant answered once, missing likewise. Reaching Jessup, Corman hunkered over the man, blasting still in an increasingly frantic effort to get on target, and suddenly his Colt began to click emptily and fume to no purpose. The captain froze momentarily, knowing that Mapes still had shots left in his cylinder, and he saw the lieutenant's evil smile as his enemy perceived that he now had the chance to stand up straight and take careful aim at his open target on the rock stairway above.

Scared, Corman swayed involuntarily from the hips as Mapes's gun flashed once more. He waited for that last instant of shocking pain or dark oblivion. But his movement had been sufficient to spoil the lieutenant's aim and the bullet did no worse than tear open Corman's coat over the left ribs and slightly burn the flesh beneath. Even so, the pain was salutary and, convinced that Mapes's next slug would pierce him dead centre, Corman dropped his revolver beside him and otherwise reacted subconsciously, snatching up two or three small lumps of rock and rising to hurl first one piece and then another at the man below.

Corman did far better here than he had with his gun. His first missile hit Mapes on the left shoulder and staggered him, while the second struck him in the middle of the chest and shook him still further. Right hand again filled, and the accurate line of flight locked into his eye, Corman went for his third throw, putting all his force behind it. His stone flew downwards, curving just enough, and it hit the lieutenant at the top of his forehead. Mapes toppled on to his back, heels kicking high and legs parted, and he lay motionless in the scree, unconscious for the minute and perhaps a lot longer.

Corman breathed again. It was some relief anyhow.

NINE

All too certain that Major Brock and his soldiery would arrive below within a few minutes, Corman snatched up and holstered his revolver, then turned over Frank Jessup's wounded body and studied the injury for a long moment. The Raftville baker had caught a bad one and no mistake. He had been shot through the chest, but the injury was low and over to the left. Corman had seen many such hurts before—indeed, just about every kind of gunshot wound imaginable—and this sort had not always been mortal if the bleeding could be stopped and expert medical help provided. But there was no expert medical help for miles, and Jessup was simply going to bleed to death if left lying as he was now.

It was another case of doing the only thing he could. Corman quickly lifted Jessup's limp frame and pitched it across his shoulders. Then, going at the remainder of the ascent like a goat, he heaved and strained his way upwards, taking crazy chances as sweat blinded him and his mind blurred. Twice he slipped in the rubble, almost losing the stocky Jessup on each occasion, and the muscles of his thighs trembled from the extreme efforts which he demanded of them; but he reached the top of the climb without incurring disaster, and virtually collapsed there—resting only a few seconds, though, before taking up his burden again and blundering out through the people clustered about him, possessed wholly by his concern for the wounded man and having no idea of where he was to end up.

Raising his head, and with eyes slitted, Corman made his way westwards into the grassy land beyond the summit. The others stayed with him, more or less running to keep up, and they all progressed doggedly for several minutes before coming to a line of oak scrub and tulip trees.

Passing through the light timber, they entered an area of what was obviously abandoned farmland. For there were broken fences around fields that were grassing over, rusting ploughshares and broken carts in a yard, a covered well that was caving in, a collapsing barn and sheds, and a tumbledown house with broken tiles, empty windows, and green mildew and yellow moss upon its outer walls. Not a prepossessing place by any means.

Yet the house was a haven of sorts, and Corman headed for it because it meant shelter. The voices of his companions babbled around him now, but he ignored them all. With his brow knitted, teeth clenched, and obeying only the force of his will, he refused to relax the latest strain that he had imposed upon himself until he had entered the farm house by its back door and lowered the still unconscious Frank Jessup on to the flagstones of the kitchen floor. Then he straightened up, reeled against a stone sink and its rusty pump, and sleeved off dazedly and gradually satisfied his starved lungs with great gulps of air.

'They'll find us here, Brad,' Anne Corman said.

'Yes,' the captain gasped, 'they'll find us here.'

'Why bring us here then?'

'You'd rather have stayed out there and kept running?'

Anne Corman jerked a shoulder helplessly.

'We might have outdistanced them,' Bill

Tidy reminded, passing down a neckerchief to use as a wound-stauncher now Jean Coltrane had gone down on her knees beside Frank Jessup and was doing what she could for him.

'My legs wouldn't have lasted much longer,' Corman said shortly. 'I know it's a poor best—but it is the best we can do for Frank Jessup. The folk from Bowie will surely show up before long. With luck, he'll be all right till then.'

'You're a great man for trusting to luck, Cap'n,' Tony Sales put in drily, the light in his black, button-bright eyes a little malicious.

'Don't you start,' Corman warned. 'Old Frank was beginning to get under my skin with talk of that sort.'

'Are we goin' to stand here and wait for it?' Bill Tidy wondered. 'That Yankee major and his scum will get here first. You must know that, Brad.'

'Hell, yes.'

'They'll kill us men.'

'Real dead,' Corman gulped, drawing his empty revolver and tipping out its fired shells—'if they get the chance.'

'So how are we goin' to stop 'em?' Tidy queried, eyeing the revolver which the captain was now reloading with cartridges from the pouch on the gunbelt that he had removed from Sergeant White's body. 'That gun of yours is now the only firearm here.'

'Leave it to me, Bill.'

'Leave it—?'

'Bill, I've been in situations not so different from this one before,' Corman said, glancing up rather disapprovingly at the holed ceiling which connected the kitchen with a bedroom on the floor above.

'We're bad outnumbered.'

'The remedy's to slim the enemy down,' the captain commented. 'Nor is the question of numbers such a vexing one any more. Even if you count Jack Mapes in, I don't reckon there can be more than eight of that renegade band left now.'

'Eight's eight.'

'One bullet is enough,' Corman admitted, taking the other's point as he eased the hammer of his pistol down and tipped the weapon into its holster. 'You and the others stay here, Bill, and watch out for yourselves. I'm going out to attend to a little business.'

'Like saving your own hide?' Tony Sales

asked in bitter disbelief.

'No,' Corman said tolerantly, 'I'm going to try to save yours.'

'Best stay here, then, and cover us with that of yours.'

'Let him go,' Bill Tidy said, exercising that shrewdness so often found in small men. 'He knows what he's gotta do, and how to do it.'

'I just hope to goodness he does,' Sales breathed grimly.

Corman neither stayed to say nor hear any more. He slipped out of the kitchen door without even a glance at anybody. Then he strode along the back of the derelict house, making for the line of tulip trees about fifty yards beyond the building. Even now he was trying to think of some better way of going to work than that which he planned, but he could not come up with one that stood any chance of being successful. Ambush, even when it was one man ambushing the many, was not a method of eliminating foemen that he liked. Yet sometimes it was necessary to deal ruthlessly with the ruthless; and this appeared to be one of those occasions. He could only defend his companions by slaying their enemies, and that he must do by any means he could.

On reaching the trees he became more cautious and, dodging among the slender trunks, soon arrived at the other side. Here he paused in the shadows of the timber and looked across the ground which he and his companions had so recently crossed. There was nobody in sight as yet, and the breeze bent the grass of the empty land towards him, light flowing through the turn of the stems and gleaming on the myriad heads of marigold and daisy. The airs swept at his face, rushing a little, and they were cool and fragrant. He recalled how he had often lain on the prairie as a kid, enjoying the vivid blue of the sky and dreaming. More than once he had heard men say that dreams long-held came true. Well, his hadn't. There had been many a moment in his life that he had not visualised—and this was another of them.

There was a boulder-pile about two hundred yards beyond him and out to his left. Other rocks of some magnitude studded the area too. He would need a wide field of fire when Major Brock and his men entered that quadrant of the land—adequate cover to protect him if he had to retreat in a hurry—and a clear path

168

by which to skirt back to the farm house if he must. Yes, that rock-heap yonder was so positioned that it met all his requirements more adequately than they were going to be met anywhere else in the vicinity.

Leaving the trees, he headed for the rock-pile which he had selected at a crouched run, drifting in behind it and praying that the renegades—always assuming that nothing of overriding importance had occurred elsewhere and they did show up—would cross the same piece of country that he and his companions had traversed as a matter of course on leaving the rim of the hollow perhaps half a mile to the east of here.

Drawing his revolver, Corman raised himself behind a corner of the rock-pile and gazed over the jagged stones at eye-level before him. His stare brooded upon the land where he expected the first threatening movements to manifest, and it was little more than a minute later when Major Brock and a sick-looking Lieutenant Mapes came into view. The officers were leading the six enlisted men that Corman had seen dismount on the campsite in the hollow, and all eyes were lowered on to what were evidently readable traces left by Corman and his party not long ago. The soldiers were pointing out details to one another, and were plainly engrossed in what they were doing. That suited the watching captain very well; for, while the men's attention was taken up by the ground beneath them, they were not going to give any thought to the possibility that they might be ambushed and ought to be easy marks when he sprang his surprise.

He allowed the enemy to pass the middle of his cover by a yard of two, thus placing them on the ground that he judged, from their standpoint, to be the furthest from shelter hereabouts. Then, thumbing his pistol on cock, he stepped round the eastern end of the rock-heap that had hidden him up to now and fired diagonally at the soldiers who had just gone by. It was done without the slightest warning, and the blast of his Colt was echoed by a shocked scream as his first victim fell, shot through the backbone. Shifting his aim, Corman let another man have it, and then a third, his surprise so complete that the impact of it completely robbed his foes of their wits and left them hapless targets who gaped round only to stop lead.

Two more men crumpled up before

Corman's pitiless shooting, and he was reminded of his first battle at the Manassas Junction when, with the Yankees licked and reduced to simple pockets of resistance, he had sat his standing horse and fired into the clustered enemy with an unfeeling determination to kill until there was nobody left on the other side to kill. The same mood was on him here, and for the same reason, because those you slew could slay no more themselves.

He got his sixth soldier. Then his hammer snapped against a fired cartridge. The cylinder of his weapon was empty. He had achieved a considerable slaughter, but his two most formidable enemies—protected from his fire by their position behind the lesser men—were still alive. But Brock and Mapes, recovered from their startlement by now, had swung on him and started shooting back. Corman would gladly have faced their fire had his gun still carried any loads, but he was now defenceless and just a target himself; so, spinning round in his turn, he shrank low and dodged back behind the boulder-pile adjacent, slanting his run after that towards another heap of stones not far away and then directing his feet—down his safest line of retreat—towards the northern end of the not far distant tulip trees. His heightened senses could already pick up the faint magnolia scent of the timber, and he felt drawn on by it, while the guns of Brock and Mapes flamed at him over every few yards of his flight, bullets missing him by inches only when not hitting piled rock and wailing off in ricochets.

Once more the trees concealed him, and now the firing ceased. He heard Jack Mapes give vent to an oath, while Brock swore at the renegade Southerner in his turn and urged the lieutenant into pursuit. Corman threw all his mind and strength into getting away. His legs scissored faster than ever, and his feet fairly flew over the ground, his soles making little sound at all. Beyond the trees he sped, then along the rear boundary of the abandoned farm property and among the tumbledown sheds at the western end of the place, checking now behind the corner of a building and slamming in hard against the ancient brickwork. Holding himself as rigid as he could, the captain listened to the harsh pumping of his lungs while he pressed his shoulder-blades against the wall behind him and slanted an eye back across the ground that he had himself just covered at such a pace. Hard as he peered, he could not make out any sign of his pursuers as yet—for there were shrubs and bits of ruined outhouses along the course that created obscurity between his present position and the tulip trees at the eastern end of the homeground—but it was only a few seconds before Brock and Mapes showed up distantly and then slowed in their strides, peering after his vanished figure and cursing in frustration and obvious bafflement at the manner in which he had so far eluded them.

The pair picked up speed and came on again, but they were perceptibly wary and had most of their attention fixed on the back door of the derelict house, which was already in their field of vision. Corman could have dropped them both had he had the bullets in his gun, but the weapon was still empty and he knew that it was vitally necessary to make his reload as soon as possible. Yet he hesitated, fearing that either one of the officers might spot his slightest movement against the wall behind the corner of the shed. In fact neither the major nor the lieutenant looked in his direction, and Corman judged that he had indeed better take this opportunity and make his reload now—for a loaded gun was all important to whatever he did next—so he opened the pouch of his military gunbelt again and took out the bullets remaining in it. These were six in number, and represented one complete recharge of the Colt's cylinder.

Corman tipped out the spent contents of his pistol; then, his fingers fumbling a trifle, filled the Colt's chambers with the new ammunition. With the weapon cocked and again an effective killing tool, he looked across the yard once more—hoping that Brock and Mapes were still in the open—but the space was empty and he was forced to assume that Brock and Mapes had entered the house during the minute that he had been occupied with his gun and Corman could only suppose that the pair now had the people who had been hiding there under the muzzle of their weapons.

It was a very unfortunate circumstance but, as things had gone, he did not see how it could have turned out otherwise. He realized that, with the women in their grasp, Brock and Mapes had achieved their most important aim. They might kill off the men at any moment. Corman felt something like a wave of despair pass over him, but he flung it off. This was no time to lose heart. The danger that things would not work out perfectly had always been implicit in his doings. He was in a constantly changing situation, but he might still be able to rescue his friends before it was too late. If he could act quickly enough and perhaps create another surprise. But he must break this inertia and get on with it. His options were few and, well aware that he wasn't far away—and wouldn't go away—Brock and Mapes would be watching for him every moment of the time.

Corman's imagination worked hard, and certainty came to him very suddenly. He must go in through the house. That shouldn't prove too difficult, since there wasn't a whole window or door left in the building. Maybe he could stick up his enemies through that hole in the kitchen ceiling. They were almost certainly functioning below it. If he could get to that spot upstairs without giving himself away, it might be done. And it was possible and even likely that the major and the lieutenant—who must be nervous men—would give no thought to the chance that they could be attacked from above and ignore any slight sound that they heard from upstairs.

Turning left, Corman threw himself into action. He raced around the walls of the shed, emerging at the front of the crumbling erection and from the side of it away from the yard. Sure that whatever movements he made here could not be seen from the back of the house, he stepped on to the open ground between the shed and the front of the mildewed dwelling, going forward until he reached an unglazed window that met him with all the malign vacancy of an eyeless socket in a skull. Putting his head into the aperture, Corman tilted his left ear towards the position of the kitchen and listened intently. He could hear voices, but only faintly, and the low volume of the sound made him reasonably certain that he could enter the dilapidated dwelling at this spot without any hint of his presence reaching his enemies.

Swinging up his left leg, the captain stepped over the windowsill and straddled it. The movement put no strain on him and he was able to draw his other leg into the building after him without raising the slightest sound. He might have paused again on the dusty floor boards beneath him—since it would have been a great help if he could have ascertained that all the other people in the house were indeed in the kitchen—but the seconds were ticking away and he had to get on; so he crossed the room in which he now found himself and halted in the doorway at its opposite side, peeping out quickly and turning his head in either direction. He realized that he was looking into the hall, which held the front door to his right and a flight of stairs on his immediate left, while the continuation of the open space beyond the steps ended at a back wall that had two doors in it, one of which appeared to serve a main room and the other a passage that probably went through into the kitchen.

Thus, with a rough idea of the building's plan on this side, Corman catfooted to the bottom of the stairs and began to tiptoe upwards. His probing feet located one or two squeaky risers and the odd larger fault—a split board being it in one case; and this he had to by-pass by taking two steps at once, but his careful climb soon brought him to the landing on the upper floor and he paused there, certain that no rumour of his ascent could have carried into the lower rooms.

Now the captain ran a calculating eye over the bedroom doors which opened off the landing's L shape, concluding that the one furthest to his left must be that which gave access to the room above the kitchen. Tiptoeing again, he passed through the entrance on which his gaze was fixed and knew at once that he had got it right, for a jagged hole showed itself at the middle of the floor and he heard voices rising through it from the room below.

Advancing his pistol as he went, Corman stepped slowly and carefully up to the aperture, too intent on what he was doing to decipher any of the words that were rising to his ears, and all at once he found himself reaching forward with his chin and straining his eyes downwards at the scene in the kitchen beneath. It could hardly be more perfect. Major Brock and Lieutenant Mapes were standing exactly in line with the tilt of his revolver, while the men and women from Raftville were all hidden from him in positions that he deemed to be on the left of the kitchen and well back from the spot where he was looking down. He could begin firing on the two officers below at this moment and be as certain as anybody could that he would be creating no risk to his friends. Altogether, the men down there had been unworthy of a challenge before and were still unworthy of one. If he gave them any kind of chance, he would only put himself at risk. It was time to start shooting again and finish this terrible business once and for all. Once Brock and Mapes were dead, he would be able to go home in the hope that his life's fighting was at last done with. It needed just two more accurate shots!

Corman eased forward that inch more, needing to balance himself correctly; but that was his undoing, for the floor suddenly broke away under his feet and pitched him into space.

TEN

The rush downwards was brief and startling. Corman could do nothing about it and hit the floor very hard indeed. Somersaulting obliquely after the impact, he just missed the legs of the two men whom he had been covering a moment before. Retaining his senses and also, as his spinning brain dimly perceived, his pistol, the thought flashed through his consciousness that he could even now win out here, for he had come to rest a little behind Brock and Mapes and had the instant that it would take them to face round in which to gather himself and bring up his gun. The other two men were obviously shocked by the suddenness of what had occurred and he should be able to fire twice before they could get into action.

Though stunned, Corman was still determined in the last degree. He began to act, and it was all going precisely as he wished, when a figure came leaping at him and the gun was kicked from his grasp and sent spinning to the further end of the room, where it struck the wall and went off with a deafening roar, the bullet flying upwards and burying itself in the ceiling.

Corman, already raised off his hips, fell back on to his right elbow and stared upwards dazedly, and it slowly got through to him that his attacker had been his own wife. Anne Corman was bending over him now with her hands upon her hips and a defiant expression in her beautiful almond shaped eyes, across which a long curl twisted in much the same rebellious spirit. 'No, Brad!' she announced, while the major and lieutenant fetched their pistols round to cover him and the expressions of relief upon their faces turned to ones of wolfish triumph. 'There is to be no more killing!'

'Are you crazy?' Corman choked at her. 'You've done no less than sign our death warrants!'

'You're wrong, Brad,' the woman said, emphatic still. 'I've made an agreement with Major Brock and Jack Mapes. If Jean Coltrane and I go along with them quietly—allowing ourselves to be used when necessary as hostages—there will be no more killing here.'

'Do you believe that?' Corman asked incredulously. 'Those two hellions only came to that agreement with you because they need to move fast and must have your co-operation. They've come on to this high grass afoot, and will need to pull off an ambush in due course to put themselves back in the saddle. They can't risk struggling females about them.'

'What of it?' Anne Corman demanded.

'They'll murder you and Jean when they've got fresh horses and have no further need of you. Dammit, woman! Those two have been getting deeper and deeper into trouble, and they're now at their wits' end! It's all fallen apart for them. They're near finished, and they'd do anything—promise anything—to get what they want. Can't you see that? Bowie will string them up, Anne, and they know it!'

'Well, I don't want to see them lynched, Brad.'

'Not after what they've done?' Corman spluttered, unable to credit that anybody could be so stupid, no matter how perverse their emotions might be with regard to the subject of their words. 'These men are murdering thieves! It's not just a case of how are the mighty fallen! These were always paltry beings—not special ones fallen from grace. In God's name, Anne!'

'Jack Mapes would never harm me,' Anne Corman said confidently. 'We've been far too much to each other. And Jack would never let the major lay a finger on me either.'

'Didn't you hear how the callous and uncaring varmint talked about you and everybody else down there in that army camp?' Corman inquired. 'Mapes cares as little for you as he does a rabbit!'

'Tell him different, Jack,' the woman requested.

'I'm telling you different, Brad,' Mapes smirked.

'See?'

'Is there anything more blind than a faithless wife?' Corman pleaded of the ceiling. 'You've been whoring while I've been fighting for the South and every dream we ever had.'

'Wasn't that your trouble?' his wife suddenly raged, obviously stung by the suggestion that she was an immoral woman who had done her husband the worst kind of wrong. 'Dreams of glory! Piffle and poppycock! You didn't want the responsibility of a home and me. All you wanted, once you'd lain with me in bed, was to ride off and fight Yankees. Youth, excitement! You wanted to taste the lot—to have your cake and eat it—to be so plain selfish and uncaring of other people's wishes that you even made your mother and father want to spew out the taste of you! Don't you dare revile me, Brad Corman! You're a hundred—and a thousand-times worse!'

'You can certainly run on,' Corman said disgustedly. 'I never heard such a rigamarole. Talk about lies and excuses. Don't you know right from wrong?'

Major Brock stamped a foot savagely on the floor. 'What the deuce are we listening to here, Mapes? Are you caught up in this mesh of words—this farrago of marital insult? I don't give a damn about their squabbles, and neither should you. No, sir! Our time's running away. How long do you think it will take those people who were back there on the ridge—having seen what they must have seen—to ride round the land and come upon us here? That gunfire of Corman's will act as guide enough.'

'You're right, Major,' Jack Mapes admitted, 'but Annie can sure lay it on when she likes. Hell, but I enjoyed listening to her! I have a place in it somewhere I guess.'

'Bite it off!' Brock snapped. 'Shoot Corman; then we can be on our way. I'll bring Mrs Coltrane along, and you can bring that paramour of yours.'

Mapes cocked his revolver. He pointed its muzzle at Corman's head. The captain waited for extinction. It seemed to him just then that all life ended in a form of betrayal.

There was a rush of footfalls from the part of the room where the people from Raftville were gathered, and Jean Coltrane's voice shouted hysterically: 'You promised no more killings, you liars!'

Corman saw Mrs Coltrane lunging at Mapes. Her body struck his and knocked the lieutenant aside. Mapes's gun went off, but the bullet intended for Corman's brain hit the floor and flattened itself there, leaving a silvery-grey smudge where it had dissipated.

There was a moment of total chaos. Corman gazed at the figures jostling before him as they tried to sort themselves out. He was possessed at once by that feeling of last chance. Swinging round, face to the flagstones, he went scuttling up the room like some impossibly fast crocodile and scooped up the revolver which his wife had kicked from his hand a few minutes ago. Twisting about once more, he dropped back into a sitting position against the room's eastern wall and saw Major Brock reach out and pull Jean Coltrane to him. The soldier instantly blew the woman's brains out, and she fell like a rag doll and lay just as untidily. Not quite fast enough to prevent the murder, Corman nevertheless got in a second later, shooting for the widest part of Brock's body. Staggering, Brock jerked erect and grunted, a scarlet stain emerging on the left breast of his blue coat, and he glowered at Corman and tried desperately to fetch his Colt into line, but the captain triggered a second time—getting his man through the heart—and Brock buckled to the floor and threshed into immobility.

The major's demise seemed to have a profound effect on Jack Mapes. Short of attempting to avenge Brock, the lieutenant made for the back door and bounded out into the farmyard, turning left and haring for the end of the house on that side. Venting a sort of agonised cry, Anne Corman went after the man, showing a turn of speed that would have left many a youth standing, and she had already disappeared from sight as her husband regained the vertical and immediately hurled himself down the room as the third presence in the pursuit.

Outside, Corman dashed for the western end of the house, skidding round it and catching a glimpse of his wife's figure, ahead of him by thirty yards and over to his right. Following the woman exactly now, Corman kicked through a pile of ancient sawdust beside the mouldering barn and found himself clear of further obstructions and looking up country. The grey clad shape of Lieutenant Mapes was in sight again from here. Mapes was still running like one possessed, and heading into the west, where a pale skyline revealed a prairie break of tumbling rock and scrub pine, as good a place to hide as any that the low, rolling country of this neighbourhood had to offer.

Mapes put in another burst. He opened up the gap between him and the two people pelting after him still more. But it couldn't last. Even the body of the fittest man could not be driven flat out for more than a few minutes. Suddenly Mapes broke stride and began to flounder, looking back and seeming to drag his face along in some peculiar fashion as he eyed both his pursuers malevolently. 'Wait for me, Jack!' Anne Corman shouted. 'Oh, wait for me.'

The lieutenant stumbled, his arms flying and his knees on the wobble, the rhythm of his flight completely broken. Anne Corman, legging it grimly, began to overhaul him, and the long-limbed Corman himself started overtaking her. Now Mapes achieved a brief recovery, but within half a minute it was apparent that the lieutenant was pretty well spun out, and when he actually tripped and fell, only to pick himself up and immediately fall again, it was evident that his flight as such was finished. 'Jack!' the pursuing Anne screamed. 'Jack—please!'

Mapes stopped. Turning, he put his knuckles on his knees and stood crouched and slavering, the blaze of madness in his eyes. Then, undoubtedly with a view to slowing Corman up, he fired his gun at the intervening woman and brought her down. Horrified, as the lieutenant began to set one foot in front of the other again, Corman ran on to where his wife lay and knelt down beside her, gripping her by the shoulders and gently tipping her on to her back. Anne's cheeks were ashen, and there was a remoteness in her staring eyes, while her brow kept wrinkling up and a froth of tiny red bubbles appeared on her lips. It was plain that her life was ebbing fast, but what remained of it kept straining in her to find some form of expression—perhaps to ask pardon, spit more defiance, or mouth some irrelevance—but Corman ignored the effort and tried to soothe her during the minute that was left. Then a spasm shook her and she passed from this life, having uttered no last word.

Too drained to feel any deep emotion about the manner of his wife's death, Corman thrust himself erect at her side and swept the land ahead with his eyes, seeking a new glimpse of the lieutenant, but Mapes was no longer in sight and must have dropped into a hiding place not too far away while Corman's attention had been fully occupied with the dying Anne. His gaze calculating, Corman measured the country before him in terms of what he judged to be the largest arc of retreat on which the fugitive could now be located; then, keeping all his senses alert and his gun at the ready, walked into the land behind the imaginary curve; for, as matters stood, an attempt to ambush him shortly was about as sure as night following day.

There was no fear in the captain. He felt only an implacable resolve to shoot fast and straight when the opportunity arrived. An icy fatalism was with him too. Men doubted—and he had often been among them—that there was justice under heaven, but in his secret heart he knew that the evil were only allowed to run their course unchecked up to a given point. Instinct told him that Mapes had reached the end of his race. He had become a mindless killer. Murder had become his only way. Such a being had to be removed from human affairs because his activities no longer served even the purposes of hell. For the devil had his logic too. This was Jack Mapes's last day. Corman was the man's appointed executioner. The captain was sure of it.

Some tufts of long grass parted a little to the right of Corman's line of advance. He picked up the tiny movement with the corner of his eyes, but didn't let the man behind the green stems know that he had been spotted. The blue steel of a gun barrel inched into view, and Mapes's face shaped up behind it, a cold orb squinting. The captain delayed no longer. He swung on the hidden man, screwing downwards over his right knee as he fired, and the other cried out and returned the compliment, jerking half erect to reveal that part of his left cheek had been shot away. Mapes was an awful sight, but still in the battle and, more by luck than judgment, he put a slug through the captain's left cuff. Steadied by the breath of hot lead, Corman gave himself that extra split second which so often made the difference, and he shot Mapes in the body. The lieutenant toppled backwards, the pistol flying from his grasp, and hit the ground with his torso slightly raised by another large tuft of grass. He lay with his lungs pumping feebly and blood streaming profusely from a wound just under his heart.

Corman closed in on his stricken enemy. He saw at once that Mapes was fatally wounded. Cocking his hammer, he prepared to despatch his man in the same unfeeling spirit that had possessed him wholly up to this point; but then some part of his nature thawed and he knew that he could not finish the lieutenant off in cold blood. If he did that, he would be no better than the killers with whom he had been dealing. 'It's finished, Jack,' he said, his words expressing what he believed to be the fact of it and the sheer relief he felt. 'You would have it.'

'It—it was her fault,' Mapes faltered, more resentment than hatred in his gaze.

'Anne's?' Corman queried. 'No. She was just the average discontented wife. What did you kill her for?'

'I—I told you.'

'No, it was pure badness, Jack—and well you know it. You didn't have to do it.'

A wicked smile had appeared on Mapes's face. It wasn't irrelevant, yet didn't seem to entirely fit in with the talk. Indeed, the dying lieutenant seemed to be looking beyond Corman and to possess an intelligence that had yet to communicate itself to the captain—who just then received his first intimation of movement at his back. But he had yet to get his head round, when the noise of a gun cocking all but paralysed him and the too well remembered voice of Rufus Lebeau asked contemptuously: 'How do you know what he did or didn't have to do, Corman?'

'Yeah,' Johnny Hiker's hectoring tones backed up. 'Ain't you the know-all, soldier? Nothing like you this side of hell. Well, maybe. But we've got you, and that's all that counts. Yeah?'

Corman could not contradict the pistolero, and his heart settled towards his boots. He felt cheated beyond words. He had done so much, dared so much, suffered so much, and been sure that the victory was his. Now this! Defeat, sudden and absolute! How could he have permitted himself to lose sight of Rufus Lebeau and John Hiker again? The only explanation was that, subconsciously, he had allowed himself to think of them as among the dead in the hollow, then let his mind shed all memory of them. It was an inexcusable thing to have done, yet he had done it—and would unquestionably soon have to pay for it.

Corman saw a figure on horseback ride out slowly from behind him. The rider was the pistolero. Hiker circled his mount, halting behind the mortally wounded Jack Mapes and facing the prisoner, his revolver cocked and pointing. For an instant Hiker tempted the gun that Corman was still holding—and the captain might well have accepted the challenge had his weapon been more fully charged—but he had only one chamber left to fire and realized that, if he should get Hiker, Lebeau would still get him when he whirled with his empty Colt and could only go through the motions, so he dropped his pistol on Hiker's command and raised his hands, waiting for the ultimate blow to fall. 'Want to do it,

Mapes?' Lebeau asked. 'You still up to it?'

'No,' the lieutenant murmured weakly. 'You see how it is with me. You got here—too late. But—but how did—did you get here at all?'

'Leave it to us!' Hiker boasted, his rat snout turned upwards and his entire expression one of self-congratulation. 'It surely was neat, eh, boss? How we pulled a smart one on them folks from Bowie? There was this kid, d'you see? He was watching a part o'the ridge the rest of the people with him couldn't see from where they were. We kind of tough-talked that boy into believin' we'd had orders to ride back to town and get in a new supply of ammunition. He fell for it, and off me and Rufus went. Hot damn!'

Mapes smiled faintly, his wound spluttering blood for a moment as his heart anticipated giving up the effort to keep him alive. 'Please me, gentlemen,' the lieutenant whispered. 'Hang the—the bastard from a tree!' Then his gaze fixed, his jaw sagged, and a last breath issued tremulously from his throat.

'He's gone,' Lebeau observed harshly. 'He didn't say a word about Major Brock and the rest.'

'They're gone too,' Corman said through his teeth.

'Sounds like you've been busy, mister,' Johnny Hiker remarked, not without a note of grudging admiration in his tones. 'Didn't I once say before? You're no mean hand with a gun.'

'So give me one,' Corman invited, knowing that he hadn't a hope in the devil's whole domain of his request being granted. 'Two against one. There you are. Is it a deal?'

'Don't make me sick, Corman!' Lebeau advised. 'Johnny.'

'What?'

'You know what. Do we give that dead man his wish?'

'Sorta give that soldier the rest of his rope?'

'Where he needs it most, yes.'

'I can leave that to you, boss.'

'Safely,' Lebeau acknowledged. 'We'll string him up. There are trees yonder.'

'Can see 'em,' Hiker said, deadly serious now. 'Only let's put a jerk in it, Rufus. That ride round the land isn't such a long one, and there could be others following. When kids talk, questions are asked pronto. C'rect?'

195

'Correct,' Lebeau conceded. 'The danger's there all right. But it takes little time to hang a man.' His horse stirred audibly. 'Move yourself, Corman!'

Corman obeyed. He walked past the dead body of Lieutenant Mapes, and on across the plain beyond, coming to thinly sprouted brush, and then the first of the timber—a mingling of scrub pine, aspens, and a type of oak—which he had seen in the near distance not so long ago.

Lebeau, bringing his horse and himself into the captain's full sight for the first time since Corman's capture, trotted in upon the trees—while his employee went on covering their prospective victim—and gave his attention to selecting the tree which he intended to use for the lynching, and he pointed to an old, gnarled oak, squat, far-spread and dying, and cast the lariat which he had been carrying upon his saddle over a bough that jutted from the bole at about eight feet above the ground. After that he adjusted the noose to the height he wished and swung down, tying the free end of the rope around the tree trunk and knotting it fast.

Then, gently rubbing his hands on the seat of his trousers, the saloonkeeper turned

196

to Corman, a strange and avid expression upon his florid features, and said: 'That's where they'll find you, Captain.'

'Twisting slowly in the wind,' Hiker added graphically, giggling almost girlishly at the thought.

'Use your rope to bind him, John,' Lebeau ordered.

Nodding, Hiker dismounted and, taking down his lariat from his pommel, ran out the noose and flicked it deftly over Corman's head, pulling tight with a sharp jerk and pinning the captain's arms. Then he made a series of turns about the prisoner's body securing the bindings at intervals as he went along and, by the time he had finished and tied his final knots, Corman could do no more than waggle his fingers behind his back.

'Nicely,' Lebeau approved. 'Let's put him on my horse.'

The two men got hold of Corman. Tilting his torso backwards, they kicked his legs apart; then, taking one each, they first swung and then propelled him into the saloonkeeper's saddle, the force of his arrival pitching him upright and forcing him to fill the stirrups for balance and support.

'Ready, soldier?' Hiker asked.

'Would you be?' Lebeau inquired.

'Don't guess I would at that, Rufus,' Hiker admitted. 'But that's the fun for us, ain't it?'

It was Lebeau's chin that gave a jerk this time. 'I'll lead the horse over to the tree, Johnny. You get on yours and come over too. Then put the noose around Corman's neck.'

'Yes, sir,' Hiker said, walking back to his horse and mounting up, while Lebeau led his mount—and the captive it supported—over to the bough where the halter waited.

Corman was abruptly filled with a wild desperation. There was in his mind a dazed uncertainty as to how he had reached this pass. He seemed to have surrendered his spirit no less than his body while Jack Mapes had lay dying. Not that there had been much that he could do about his capture—and he had been closely under the gun ever since—but it seemed to him that his brain had become paralysed and that his normally defiant nature had done little more than concur with all that had been done to him. But he was himself again, and did not intend to die that tamely. No, sir! There was a kick left in him, and this horse was going to get it. If the brute should get up on its hind legs and do some damage to Rufus Lebeau in the process, it would be all to the good, and he, Corman would go kiting into eternity much the happier for it.

The captain gathered his entire strength in his legs. Then he opened his feet on either side of the mount's barrel and fetched his heels inwards again with an extreme violence that he had never practised on a mount before. His rowels cut through the creature's hide and tore deep into the flesh beneath, and blood and skin flew as the horse vented a frightful screaming neigh and went rearing aloft, its fore hooves cycling madly and its jaws gnashing.

Lebeau was taken completely by surprise. He threw up his arms to protect himself There was a look of horror upon his features as the front half of the brute's body came crashing down from the considerable height to which its head had risen and its fore hooves smashed down on his skull, bursting it open like the shell of an egg. Lebeau fell, brained, while Corman, already rocketing from the saddle, reached his highest trajectory and plummeted to earth, where he lay bruised and winded but otherwise unhurt.

Still sounding off in terror, the hideously abused horse went galloping away, while Johnny Hiker, stiff in his saddle and gaping like a fool, rode slowly over to where Lebeau lay. He stared down at the man's shattered skull, then angled a bemused glance at Corman and said: 'He's dead. My, my—old Rufus is dead! You've gone and killed my boss, you polecat!' He spat, seemingly offended by the sight of blood and brain tissue oozing from Lebeau's ruined skull. 'For that, soldier, I'm going to shoot you right now!'

It was about what Corman had expected, and he had no doubt that Hiker was going to do exactly what he had said; but the badman had still to bring his weapon round and pull the trigger, when a rifle cracked some distance away and the bullet swept the pistolero off his mount, leaving him dead and curiously frail-looking on the red-spattered grass.

A minute or two went by. Then a party of folk who could only have come from Bowie came riding up. Mary Forbes and

Sergeant-major Gilhooley were in the lead. For all the recent wear-and-tear, Mary looked a treat and was holding almost upright upon her saddle a Henry rifle from whose barrel a little smoke still curled. Hank Gilhooley appeared his usual large and amiable self, and he saluted Corman, who nodded back from his undignified position on his backside and asked to be cut free. Gilhooley and Mary sprang down from their saddles and ran over to him and, using a shut-knife, the sergeant-major cut his bonds with two or three slashes. 'Obliged to you, Gilhooley,' Corman said laconically. 'Man, you were damned nearly late on parade!'

''Fraid so, Cap'n,' Gilhooley admitted. 'Sure an' it was nip-and-tuck all right. Trouble was, as you might say, we didn't know what to expect, following Lebeau and his man. Thank God Miss Forbes can shoot how she does! We could have used her one or two places you and me touched. In the name of our dear lost South.'

'God damn the Union!' Corman agreed heavily, a grave eye upon Mary Forbes.

She looked back at him no less seriously. 'We found Anne lying back there,' she said. 'I'm so sorry, Brad.'

'Don't be,' he advised. 'Not on my account. It was a false start, Mary. No kind of marriage worth mentioning.'

'I see.'

'I'll tell you about it when we have time.'

'It will be better the second time round,' Mary promised.

Corman smiled at her. He had half an idea he knew what she meant. Yes, it would be all right next time round. He was sure of it himself. And in being certain of that, he was sure of everything.

The publishers hope that this book has given you enjoyable reading. Large Print Books are especially designed to be as easy to see and hold as possible. If you wish a complete list of our books, please ask at your local library or write directly to: Dales Large Print Books, Long Preston, North Yorkshire, BD23 4ND, England.

This Large Print Book for the Partially sighted, who cannot read normal print, is published under the auspices of

THE ULVERSCROFT FOUNDATION

Other DALES Western Titles In Large Print

ELLIOT CONWAY
The Dude

JOHN KILGORE
Man From Cherokee Strip

J. T. EDSON
Buffalo Are Coming

ELLIOT LONG
Savage Land

HAL MORGAN
The Ghost Of Windy Ridge

NELSON NYE
Saddle Bow Slim

MARK DONOVAN
A Colt For A Railroad